"There's [barcode] **n us from the firs**

"Whether [obscured] **out, only** time will [obscured] **east we can admit to what we're** feeling right now and go on from here."

A tortured look entered her eyes. "We can't go on. This has to end tonight and you know it."

"Tonight—"

He searched the depths of her eyes. "We've only just begun, and we have three more precious days and nights together. How can you say it has to end now? How do we do that, Tracy?"

"Because we can't afford to start something we can't finish."

"Who says we can't?" he cried fiercely. "It already started Friday evening. Don't you know I don't ever want you to go home?"

Dear Reader,

In my latest trilogy, Daddy Dude Ranch, three injured veterans have opened up a dude ranch in the Teton Valley of Wyoming to honor the families of fallen soldiers. Their wish is to be substitute daddies for a week to one child at a time. In this first book, *The Wyoming Cowboy*, you'll meet guilt-ridden Carson, who survived his tour of duty yet felt he'd abandoned his grandfather when he went to war. He meets the heartbroken Baretta family, suffering from the loss of their husband and father. Together the three of them begin to heal. Enjoy their journey to a life of happiness and fulfillment none of them knew was awaiting them at the beginning.

Rebecca Winters

The Wyoming Cowboy
REBECCA WINTERS

HARLEQUIN® AMERICAN ROMANCE®

Recycling programs
for this product may
not exist in your area.

ISBN-13: 978-0-373-75455-7

THE WYOMING COWBOY

HARLEQUIN®

Printed in U.S.A.

www.Harlequin.com

ABOUT THE AUTHOR

Rebecca Winters, whose family of four children has now swelled to include five beautiful grandchildren, lives in Salt Lake City, Utah, in the land of the Rocky Mountains. With canyons and high alpine meadows full of wildflowers nearby, she never runs out of places to explore. These spaces, plus her favorite vacation spots in Europe, often end up as backgrounds for her romance novels. Writing is her passion, along with her family and church. Rebecca loves to hear from readers. If you wish to email her, please visit her website, www.cleanromances.com.

Books by Rebecca Winters

HARLEQUIN AMERICAN ROMANCE

*Undercover Heroes

I want to dedicate this series to the courageous men and women serving in our armed forces, who've willingly put their lives in harm's way to keep the rest of us safe. God bless all of you.

Chapter One

MARCH 1
Pulmonary Unit
Walter Reed National Military Medical Center
Bethesda, Maryland

Carson Lundgren was sitting in the hospital ward's common room watching the final moments of the NASCAR race when he heard a disturbance. Annoyed, he turned his head to see Dr. Rimer passing out a document to the eight vets assembled. What in blazes was going on?

"Ray? You're closest to the TV. Would you mind shutting it off?"

Ray nodded and put an end to one of the few distractions the men looked forward to.

"Thank you. You'll all be going home tomorrow, so I urge you gentlemen to read this and take what you can from it to heart. It's a good letter written by a former serviceman. I like a lot of things it says. While you're doing that, I'll go find our special guest and bring him in."

Special guest?

The guys eyed each other with resignation. Who

knew how long this would take? They were all anxious to watch the end of the race. Carson looked down to scan the page.

Consider how different and difficult it is to go from a life of service, where every day has a mission, and someone depends on you to make life-and-death decisions, to a life with civilians who are making decisions about what client to call back first or what is the best outfit to wear to work.

Life would be different, all right. In Carson's case he didn't need to worry about choosing the proper clothes. He was going back to his Wyoming ranch, where a shirt and jeans had been his uniform before he'd signed up for the Marines. It would be his uniform again, now that he was out of the service.

In the beginning it feels as if you are so much more experienced than the people around you, and in a lot of ways you are. But that kind of thinking will only further alienate you from others. Practicing humility is the best possible advice I can give to help with reintegration into civilian life.

Carson did feel more "experienced." He'd seen things in the war that he could never explain to people who hadn't gone through the same thing.

Veterans need to recognize that even a short tour in a combat zone can have an effect on them.

While it takes everyone some time to recover after coming home, those who have seen, or been directly affected by a traumatic or horrific event (using your own definition or a generally accepted definition of such an event), need to be able to reconcile that it may have an impact on their lives and relationships with others after the deployment is over.

Since Carson had no family and his grandfather was dead, he didn't need to worry about that.

Seeking help is not a sign of weakness, no more than asking your buddy to cover your backside. The body may heal from scars and wounds readily, but the scars and wounds of trauma can last much longer and are more difficult to heal.

Difficult? A caustic laugh escaped from him. The cough he'd developed in Afghanistan would never go away, and no one could convince him otherwise.

I promise that, in time, you will see that your civilian counterparts are skilled and have a perspective that you may not have ever considered. And through a respect for what they do and what they have done, you will learn that you, too, are valued and respected.

Carson had always respected the ranch staff and knew he could count on their support.

Just as you are on edge in the beginning, they too may be a little unsure of how to treat you and how to act around you.

They'd treat him just the same as always.

So, take the first step. Be patient, be kind and be humble, and you will see that the transition is much easier.

"Gentlemen?" Dr. Rimer came back in the room where most of them were coughing because of the same affliction. He was followed by a five-star general decked out in full-dress uniform. Carson glanced at his buddies, Ross and Buck, wondering what was going on.

"I'm pleased and honored to introduce General Aldous Cook. He's anxious to talk to you men recovering in the unit. He's been asked to do some investigating for the Senate committee examining the troubling findings of the *Millennium Cohort Study of 2009*."

The eight of them got to their feet and saluted him before shaking his hand.

The General smiled. "Be seated, gentlemen. I'm honored to be in your presence and want to thank you for your invaluable service to our country." He cleared his throat. "I understand you're all going home tomorrow and have a great deal on your minds so I'll make this quick.

"As you're well aware, a significant number of returning American veterans like yourselves have reported respiratory problems that started during deployment to Iraq and Afghanistan. The study of 2009 revealed that fourteen percent of the deployed troops reported new breathing problems, compared with ten percent among those who hadn't deployed.

"Though the percentage difference seems small when extrapolated for the two million troops who've been deployed since 2001, the survey suggested that at least 80,000 additional soldiers have developed post-deployment breathing problems.

"There's a fierce debate under way over just how long-lasting and severe these problems really are. We're tracking the numbers accrued among the troops based in Southern Afghanistan since 2009, particularly the Marines.

"After ruling out other factors, it's apparent that the powerful dust storms, plus the fine dust from metals, toxins and burn pits used to incinerate garbage at military bases, are the potential culprits. Steps need to be taken to reduce the hazards, and I'm concerned that this exposure isn't getting the serious review it needs.

"Dr. Rimer has indicated you've all improved since you've been here, but we'll continue to track your progress. He assures me that with time, most of you will overcome your coughing and shortness of breath."

Tell us another fairy tale, General.

"My concern is that every one of you receives the post-deployment care you need for as long as you need it. I'm fighting for you in the congressional hearings."

Along with the others, Carson stood up and applauded. At least the General had bothered to come to the hospital in person and make an attempt to get at the root of the problem. Carson admired him for that. The General chatted with each of them for a few minutes, then left. With the end of the NASCAR race now missed, everyone left the lounge except Carson and his two roommates, Ross and Buck.

They hadn't known each other until six weeks ago, when the three of them had been flown here from their various divisions and diagnosed with acute dyspnea. But even if they were hacking, coughing and wheezing, at least they'd arrived at the hospital on their own two feet. It tore them up that some of their buddies—especially those who'd been married with families—hadn't made it through the war.

The behavioral psychologist who'd been working with them suggested that, once they were discharged, they should find a positive way to work through their survivor's guilt.

In addition to the guilt Carson already struggled with for personal reasons, he was barely functioning. During the long hours of the night when they couldn't sleep, they'd talked about the wives and children who'd lost husbands and fathers from their own squads. If the three of them could think of a way to help those families, maybe they could forgive themselves for coming home alive.

At one point in their nocturnal discussions, Carson threw out an idea that began to percolate and gain ground. "What if we invited the fatherless kids to my ranch for a summer vacation? The ranch has lots of outdoor activities for kids who may not have spent much time out-of-doors. We could take them fishing and camping, not to mention horseback riding and hiking."

Ross sat up in his bed. "All of those are good confidence builders. Heaven knows those children will have lost some confidence. How many kids are you talking about?"

"I don't know."

"Do you have enough room for guests?"

"No. We'd have to live in the ranch house, so that wouldn't work. We'd have to put up some cabins."

"I could build them with your help," Buck offered. "Construction is what I was raised to do."

"I'm afraid I don't have much money."

Buck said, "I have a little I've put away."

"I have some, too," Ross chimed in. "Looking down the road, we'd have to hire and pay a cook and provide maid service."

Encouraged, Carson said, "No matter what, we'll have to start out small."

"Their moms will have to bring them."

"You're right, Buck. How long should they come for?"

"This is a bit of an experiment, so how about we try a week with one family and see how it goes?"

"For working mothers, I think a week sounds about right," Ross theorized. "One thing we can do is help the kids if they need to talk about death, since we've been through a lot of grief counseling ourselves."

"Good point. That's one thing we know how to do. What ages are we talking about?"

"I'm thinking about my nieces and nephews," Buck murmured. "How about little guys who are really missing their dads? Like six on up to maybe ten."

Carson nodded. "That sounds about right. They'd be school age. Younger than six might be too young."

"Agreed," they all concurred.

Before long, enthusiasm for the project they envisioned wouldn't let them alone. They soon found themselves plotting to turn Carson's ranch into a dude ranch where tourists could come along with the families of fatherless children. They would establish a fund to take care of the costs. If their pilot program went well through the summer, they'd talk about keeping it open year-round.

Their plan was a good one and sounded feasible, except for one thing. None of them had gone home yet. Anything could happen when Buck and Ross were reunited with their families. Their parents had dreams for them when their beloved sons returned to their former lives. For that reason, Carson wasn't holding his breath—what little he had at the moment. He had to admit the inhalers were helping. When he'd first been brought in, he'd been gasping for every breath and thought each was his last.

Of the three men, Carson was the only one who didn't have living family. The grandfather who'd raised him had passed away five months ago of a surprise heart attack, leaving the ranch and its problems to him. Not even his grandfather's doctor had seen it coming. Carson had flown home on emergency family leave to bury him.

In that regard, he wouldn't have to run their brainchild past the older man he'd abandoned when he'd entered the military. At the time he hadn't seen it as abandonment. They'd corresponded and phoned whenever possible, but in the end Carson wasn't there for his grandfather when the chips were down. Now it was too late to make it up to the man he'd loved.

"Tomorrow's the big day, guys." Once they were all discharged from the hospital in the morning, he knew anything could happen to change his friends' focus.

Buck nodded. "I'll join you before the week is out."

Maybe. But knowing Buck was the oldest son in a large, close-knit family who wanted and needed him back in the construction business, maybe not. "Give me a call and I'll pick you up at the airport. What about you, Ross?"

"Three days at the most."

"You think?"

He eyed him narrowly. "I *know*."

Put like that, Carson could believe him, but his family who'd made their mark in oil for generations would have its way of pressuring the favorite son who'd made it home from the war. His politician father had long laid hopes for him set in stone. Time would tell if their master plan would get off the ground.

"I can hear the carts arriving with our dinner. Let's get back to the room and eat before our final session with the shrink."

It couldn't come soon enough for any of them. The war had been their world for a long time. Tomorrow they'd leave it forever. But fear clutched him in the gut that it would never leave them.

MAY 2
Sandusky, Ohio

AT THREE O'CLOCK, Tracy Baretta left her office to pick up Johnny from elementary school. When she joined the line of cars waiting for the kids to come out, she hoped she'd see Clara Brewster. Her son, Nate, was a cute boy who'd invited Johnny to his birthday party last month. Johnny hadn't wanted to go, but Tracy had made him.

Maybe Nate would like to come home with her and Johnny to play, but she didn't see him or his mom. Her disappointment changed to a dull pain when she had to wait until all the kids had been picked up before her skinny, dark-haired first grader exited the school doors alone.

He purposely hung back from the others. His behavior had her worried sick. She'd been setting up some playdates with a few of the other boys in his first-grade class, but they hadn't worked out well.

Johnny preferred to be alone and stay home with her after school. He'd become a very quiet child since Tony's death and was way too attached to her. The psychologist told her to keep finding ways to get him to interact with other kids and not take no for an answer, but she wasn't gaining ground.

He got in the rear seat with his backpack and strapped himself in. She looked over her shoulder at him. "How was school today, honey?"

"We had a substitute."

"Was she fun?"

"It was a man. I didn't like him."

She eyed him in the rearview mirror. "Why do you say that?"

"He made me sit with Danny."

"Isn't he a nice boy?"

"He calls me squirt."

His tear-filled voice brought out every savage maternal instinct to protect him. Praying for inspiration she said, "Do you want to know something?"

"What?"

"Your father was one of the shortest kids in his class when he was your age. By high school he was five feet ten." The perfect size for Tracy. "That'll happen to you, too. Do you think your father was a squirt?"

"No," he muttered.

"Then forget what Danny said. When we go to Grandma's house, she'll show you lots of pictures to make you feel better."

Of course Johnny couldn't forget. Silence filled the car for the rest of the drive home to their small rental house. She parked in front of the garage. While he scrambled out of the back, she retrieved the mail and they entered through the front door.

Once inside, he raced for the kitchen. "Wash your hands before you eat anything!" He was always hungry for sweets after school.

While her six-year-old grumbled and ran into the bathroom, Tracy went to the kitchen and poured him a glass of milk before she sorted through the mail, mostly ads and bills. Among the assortment she saw a handwritten envelope addressed to Mrs. Anthony Baretta. It had a Jackson, Wyoming, postmark.

She didn't know anyone in Wyoming. Her glance took in the return address. Lundgren's Teton Valley Dude Ranch was printed inside the logo of a mountain peak.

A dude ranch? She'd heard of them all her life, but she'd never been to one. Truth be told, she'd never traveled west of the Mississippi. Every trip had been to Florida, the East Coast, New York City, the Jersey Shore or Toronto. Tony had promised Johnny that when he got out of the service next year, they'd take a big driving trip west, all the way to Disneyland. Another pain shot through her.

She took a deep breath, curious to know who would be writing to her from Wyoming. After slitting the envelope open, she pulled out the handwritten letter.

Dear Mrs. Baretta,
My name is Carson Lundgren. You don't know me
from Adam. I served as a marine in Afghanistan
before I got out of the service.

The word Afghanistan swam before her eyes. *Tony.*
She closed them tightly to stop the tears and sank down
on one of the kitchen chairs. Her husband had been
gone eleven months, yet she knew she would always
experience this crushing pain when she thought of him.

"Mom? Can I have a peanut-butter cookie?" He'd
drunk his milk.

"How about string cheese or an apple instead?"

"No-o," he moaned.

"Johnny—" she said in a firm voice.

"Can I have some for dinner?"

"If you eat everything else first."

"Okay." She heard him rummage in the fridge for the
cheese before he left the kitchen to watch his favorite
afternoon cartoons.

When he'd disappeared into the living room, she
wiped her eyes and continued reading.

Buck Summerhays and Ross Livingston, former
marines, are in business with me on the Teton
Valley Dude Ranch. We put our heads together
and decided to contact the families of the fallen
soldiers from our various units.

Your courageous husband, Anthony Baretta,
served our country with honor and distinction.
Now, we'd like to honor him by offering you and
your son John an all-expenses-paid, one-week va-

*cation at the dude ranch anytime in June, July or
August. We'll pay for your airfare and any other
travel expenses.*

Tracy's eyes widened in total wonder.

*You're welcome to contact your husband's divi-
sion commander. His office helped us obtain your
address. If you're interested and have questions,
please phone our office at the number below.
We've also listed our website. Visit it to see the
brochure we've prepared. We'll be happy to email
you any additional information.*

*Please know how anxious we are to give some-
thing back to you after Anthony's great sacrifice.
With warmest regards,
Carson Lundgren*

His words made her throat swell with emotion. With
the letter still open, she phoned the commander's office
and learned that the offer was completely legitimate.
His assistant had nothing but praise for such a worthy
cause and hoped she and her son would be able to take
advantage of it.

Tracy's thoughts flew to her plans for the summer.
When school was out, it was decided she and Johnny
would spend six weeks in Cleveland with Tony's parents. They saw Tony in their grandson and were living
for a long visit. So was Tracy, who'd been orphaned at
eighteen and had no other family.

Luckily, she had June and the first half of July off
from her job as technology facilitator for the Sandusky

school district. Both she and Johnny needed a huge dose of family love, and they would get it. Grandma planned for them to stay in Tony's old room with all his stuff. Johnny would adore that.

The Barettas were a big Italian-American family with aunts, uncles and lots of cousins. Two of Johnny's uncles were policemen and the other three were firefighters, like their father. *Like Tony, before he'd joined the Marines to help pay for a college education.*

Their loving kindness had saved her life, and Johnny's, when news of the tragedy had come. He needed that love and support more than ever. She wondered what his reaction would be when he heard what this new invitation was about.

But before she did anything else, she called her sister-in-law Natalie to feel her out. When Tracy read her the letter, Natalie cried, "You've got to be kidding me! A dude ranch? Oh, my gosh, Tracy. You'll have the time of your life. Ask Ruth. She went to one in Montana with my folks a few years ago. Remember?"

"Vaguely."

"Yeah. It was a working ranch and they helped feed animals and went on trail rides and stuff. She got to help herd some cows."

"I don't think this is that kind of a ranch, but I don't know for sure. The thing is, Johnny's been difficult for so long, I don't think he'd even like the idea of it."

"If you want, I'll tell Cory about it. I could have him call Johnny and tell him he's thinks it would be super cool."

"That might work. Johnny loves Cory and usually goes along with anything his favorite cousin says."

"Cory will want to go with him. But seriously, Tracy, I can't believe what a wonderful thing these ex-marines have decided to do. You hear a lot of talk about remembering our fallen heroes, but this is the first time I've heard of a group of soldiers doing something like this."

"I know. Believe me, I'm blown away by this letter. If Tony knew, he'd be so touched." The tears came. She couldn't stop them. "There's just one problem. The folks are expecting Johnny and me to visit there as soon as school is out. Since my vacation is over in mid-July, I would have to make arrangements to do this trip before then."

"True." Natalie's voice trailed. "It will cut into the time you planned with Mom and Dad Baretta."

"Yes. You know how they're looking forward to spending time with Johnny."

"Well, don't say anything to them until you find out if he wants to go."

"You're right. First things first. I'll let you know what happens. Thanks for being there and being my best friend."

"Ditto to you. *Ciao.*"

Deciding there was no time like the present to find out, Tracy picked up the letter and walked into the living room. Johnny was spread out on the floor with his turtle pillow-pet watching *Tom and Jerry*.

"Honey, do you mind if I shut off the TV? There's something I want to talk to you about."

He turned to look at her out of eyes as dark a brown as Tony's. She picked up the remote and turned the set off before sitting down on the couch. "We just got an invitation in the mail to do something we've never done before. It was sent by some men who used to be marines, like your father."

That seemed to pique his interest enough to sit up cross-legged. "Are they going to have a party?" In his child's world, an invitation meant a party. Since Tony's death he'd shied away from them. He seemed to have lost his confidence. It killed her.

"No. Let me read this to you."

He sat quietly until she'd finished. "What's a dude ranch?"

"It's a place to go horseback riding and probably lots of other things."

Her son had never been on a horse. Neither had she. "You mean like a cowboy?" She nodded. "Where is it?"

"In Wyoming."

"Where's that?"

"If you're interested, I'll show you on the computer."

"Okay."

He followed her into her bedroom where she had her laptop. In a second she'd brought up a map of the United States. "We live here, in Ohio." She pointed to Cleveland. "Now, watch my finger. You have to cross Indiana, Illinois, Iowa and South Dakota to get to Wyoming, right here."

She could hear his mind working. "How long would we be gone?"

"A week."

"That's a long time." His voice wobbled. "I don't want to go."

Tracy had been afraid of that answer, but she understood. It meant leaving the only security he'd ever known. Going to stay with his aunt Natalie and play with his cousin Cory, or having an overnighter on the weekend with his grandparents, who only lived an hour away, was different.

"We don't have to. These men know your daddy died and they'd like to do something nice for you, but it's your decision, Johnny. Before I turn off the computer, would you like to see some pictures Mr. Lundgren sent so you could see what it looks like?"

He sighed. "I guess."

Tracy typed in the web address and clicked. Up popped a colored photograph of the Teton Mountain Range with a few pockets of snow. The scene was so spectacular she let out a slight gasp. In the bottom of the picture was the layout of the Teton Valley Dude Ranch surrounded by sage.

A "whoa" from Johnny told her his attention had been captured. She read the description below the picture out loud.

"The dude ranch is located along the legendary Snake River in the shadow of the magnificent Teton Mountain Range. It's just five miles from the town of Jackson, a sophisticated mountain resort. Fifteen minutes away are world-class skiing areas.

"This 1,700-acre ranch operates as a cattle ranch with its own elk and deer herds, eagles and bears. There's fishing along the three miles of the Snake. At elevations from 6,200 to 7,300 feet, summers bring average temperatures of eighty degrees and low humidity.

"Mountaineering, fly-fishing, white-water rafting, wildlife expeditions, horseback riding, photo safaris, hiking and camping trips, stargazing, bird watching, ballooning, a visit to the rodeo, are all included when you stay on the ranch. Among the amenities you'll enjoy are a game room, a swimming pool, a babysitting service, laundry services and the use of a car for local transportation."

Johnny nudged her. "What's white water?"

She'd been deep in thought. "There's a picture here of some people in a raft running the rapids. Take a look."

His eyes widened. "You mean we'd do that if we went there?"

"If we wanted to."

He looked up at her. "When would we go?"

So he *was* interested. She felt a sudden lift of her spirits. "How about as soon as school is out? After our trip is over, we'll fly back to Cleveland and stay with Grandma and Grandpa for a month. Why don't you think about it, and let me know tonight before you go to bed?"

"Can I see the rest of the pictures?"

"Sure. You know how to work the computer. While you do that, I'm going to start dinner." With her fingers crossed, she got up from her swivel chair so he could sit and look at everything. He needed something to bring him out of his shell. Maybe a trip like this would help.

A half hour later he came running into the kitchen where she'd made spaghetti. "Mom—you should see the elks. They have giant horns!"

"You mean antlers."

"Oh, yeah. I forgot."

She hunkered down and gave him a hug. "It's pretty exciting stuff, huh."

He stared at her with a solemn expression. "Do you want to go?"

Oh, my precious son. "If *you* do."

JUNE 7
Jackson, Wyoming

IT WAS LATE Friday afternoon when the small plane from Salt Lake City, Utah, started to make its descent. The pilot came on over the intercom. "Ladies and gentlemen, you're about to land at the only commercial airport located inside a U.S. national park."

Johnny reached for Tracy's hand.

"We're flying over the Greater Yellowstone region with forests, mountains, wilderness areas and lakes as far as the eye can see. Ahead is the majestic Teton Range. You'll see the Snake River and the plains around it in a patchwork of colors."

Tracy found it all glorious beyond description, but when the Grand Teton came into view, knifing into the atmosphere, every passenger was struck dumb with awe.

"If you'll look below, we're coming up on Jackson Hole."

Seeing it for the first time, Tracy could understand the reason for its name. It was a narrow valley surrounded by mountains and probably presented a challenge for the pilot to land safely. She clung to Johnny's hand. Before long, their plane touched down on the tarmac and taxied to the gate.

After it came to a stop, she unclasped their seat belts. "Are you all right, honey?"

He nodded. "That was scary."

"I agree, but we're here safe and sound now." She reached for her purse above the seat. "Let's go."

They followed the other eight passengers out the exit to the tiny terminal. The second they entered the one-story building, she heard a deep male voice call her name.

Tracy looked to her left and saw a tall, lean cowboy in jeans and a Western shirt. With his hard-muscled physique, he stood out from everyone else around him. This was no actor from a Western movie set. From his well-worn black Stetson to his cowboy boots, everything about him shouted authentic.

Johnny hugged her side. "Who's that?" he whispered.

The thirtyish-looking stranger must have heard him because he walked over and reached out to shake Johnny's hand. "My name's Carson Lundgren. I'm the man who sent your mom the letter inviting you to the ranch. You have to be John." His eyes traveled over Tracy's son with a compassion she could feel.

He nodded.

"Have you found your stomach yet, or is it still up in the air?" His question made Johnny laugh. He couldn't have said anything to break the ice faster. "I'll tell you a secret. When I was your age and my grandpa took me on my first plane ride around the Teton Valley, I didn't find my stomach for a week, but you get used to it."

While her son was studying him in amazement, his hot blue gaze switched to Tracy. Her medium height meant she had to look up at him. He removed his hat, revealing a head of dark blond hair, attractively disheveled.

"Mrs. Baretta, it's a pleasure to meet you and your son."

"We're excited to be here, Mr. Lundgren, and honored by the invitation. Please call us Johnny and Tracy."

"Terrific. You can call me Carson." He coughed for a

few seconds. "Forgive me. I do that quite often. Something I picked up overseas. It's not contagious."

Johnny's head tipped back to look at him. "You used to be a marine like my dad, huh?"

"Yup. I have a picture of him and his buddies." He pulled a wallet from his pocket. Inside was a small packet of photos. He handed one to Johnny. "I didn't know him, because I'd just been transferred in from another detail when the picture was taken. But I learned Tony Baretta came from a long line of firefighters and had the reputation of being the toughest marine in the unit. You can keep it."

"Thanks." His young voice trembled. "I loved him."

"Of course you did, just like I loved my grandpa."

"What about your dad?"

"My parents were killed in a freak flood when I was a baby. My grandparents raised me. After my grandma died, it was just Grandpa and me."

"Didn't you have cousins?"

"Nope. How about you?"

He looked at Tracy. "How many do I have, Mom?"

"Let me think. Twenty-two-and-a-half at the present counting."

Carson's brows lifted. "You're lucky. I would have given anything for just one."

That sounded like a lonely statement. Tracy looked over Johnny's shoulder while he studied the photograph. She counted a dozen soldiers in uniform. When she found Tony, her eyes glazed over.

Johnny's next remark surprised her because it wasn't about his father. "You look different in a helmet."

"We were just a bunch of metal heads." Johnny

laughed again. "None of us liked them much, but the gear kept us protected."

"I like your cowboy hat better," Johnny said before putting the picture in his pocket.

Carson grinned. The rugged rancher was one striking male. "Shall we get you a hat like it on our way to the ranch?"

"Could we?" Tracy hadn't seen him exhibit this kind of excitement in over a year.

"Of course. You can't live on a dude ranch without your duds."

"What are duds?"

"Everything I'm wearing plus a lot of other things."

"What other things?"

"Chaps and gloves for bull riding."

"Do you ride *bulls?*" Johnny's eyes grew huge.

"I used to when I was training for the rodeo."

"Can I see one?"

"Sure. I'm planning on taking you to the Jackson rodeo on the last night you're here. You'll see barrel racing and steer wrestling too."

"Mom!" Johnny cried out with uncontained excitement.

"Come on, partner. Let's get your luggage and we'll go shopping."

"As long as you let me pay for everything," Tracy interjected.

He shook his head. "While you're here, we take care of everything for the kids."

"I can't allow that," she insisted. "A free vacation is one thing, but I'll be buying whatever Johnny wants or needs while we're here."

His blue eyes flickered before he shoved his hat back on. "Yes, ma'am."

Johnny had to hurry to keep up with the larger-than-life cowboy whose long powerful legs reached the baggage claim in a few strides.

"I bet you're hungry. Do you like buffalo burgers?"

"Buffalo?"

Tracy tried to hide her smile. Her son turned to her. "Mom? Are there really buffalo burgers?"

"Yes, but I've never eaten one."

He looked at Carson. "Are they good?"

"Do you like hamburgers?"

"Yes."

"Then you don't have anything to worry about." His lips twitched when he glanced at Tracy. "Which bags are yours?"

"The two blue ones and the matching shoulder bag."

"Here you go." He handed Johnny the shoulder bag and he reached for the other two. "The van's right outside." Her son had to be surprised, but she noticed he carried the bag like a man and kept up with Carson.

They walked outside into a beautiful, still evening. She loved the dry air, but could tell they were at a much higher elevation than they were used to. The mountain range loomed over the valley, so close she felt dwarfed by it.

Their host shot her a concerned glance. "Are you all right, Tracy?"

"I'm fine."

"The air's thinner than you're used to in Ohio."

"It isn't that as much as the mountains. They're so close to us, I feel like they're pressing in."

"I had the same feeling in reverse when we reached

Afghanistan and I got off the plane with no mountains in sight where we landed. I felt like I was in a constant state of free-fall. Without landmarks, it took me a while to get my bearings."

"Coming from a paradise like this, I can't even imagine it. Tony and I grew up on Lake Erie. He told me that after he got there, with no water in sight, he went into shock."

"We all did," Carson murmured. "On every level."

She hadn't talked to anyone about Tony's war experiences in a long time and hadn't wanted to. But this was different, because Carson had made a connection by being there, too. With that photo in his pocket, her son wouldn't forget, either.

He guided them to the dark green van. It was easy to spot, with the same logo on the side she'd seen on the envelope. He stowed their luggage in the rear, then helped her and Johnny into the backseat.

"First we'll head to the Silver Dollar Grill for some grub."

"What's grub?"

"That's what the ranch hands call food. After that, we'll drive over to the Boot Corral and get you outfitted. I think they even sell some mustangs."

"What are those?"

"Cap guns. When I was little I had a mustang and played like I was Hopalong Cassidy."

"Who was he?"

"Hoppy was a straight shooter and my favorite cowboy."

His dark head jerked around to Tracy. "Did you ever see Hoppy?"

Her quick-study son was soaking up all this fascinating information like a sponge. "When I was a little girl my father had some old Western movies and we'd watch them. Hoppy was the good guy who always played fair. He had white hair and wore a black cowboy hat."

"Hey—" He looked at Carson. "So do you!" Johnny cried in delight.

"Yup. I wanted to be just like him."

Tracy smiled. "He had two partners. One old duffer was called Gabby, and the young one was called Lucky. I was crazy about Lucky. He was tall and good-looking."

Johnny giggled.

"All the girls loved Lucky," Carson commented. "That was mushy stuff."

"Yeah," her son agreed with him.

"Now we know where Lucky got his name, don't we." Carson winked at her. "I have a couple of old Western movies on CD, and you can see him in action."

"Can we watch it tonight?"

"No, young man," Tracy intervened. "When we get to the ranch, we're both going straight to bed. It's been a long day."

"Your mom's right, Johnny. Tonight we'll load you up with one of those mustangs Hoppy used to use and all the ammo you want. In a few days, when I take you out riding, we'll scout for bad guys."

"I've never been on a horse."

"Never?"

"No."

Those blue eyes flicked to Tracy. "How about you?"

She shook her head. "I'm afraid we're a pair of the greenest greenhorns you ever met. When I saw your dude ranch logo on the envelope, I never dreamed Johnny and I would end up spending time on one."

His chuckle slid in under the radar to resonate through her. "With a couple of lessons that problem will be rectified and you can explore to your heart's content. There's no place like it on Earth. My grandfather used to tell me that, but it wasn't until I came home for his funeral last November that I realized what he meant." She heard the tremor in his voice.

He'd had a recent loss, too. Tracy sensed he was still suffering.

Carson broke their gaze and looked back at Johnny. "We have four ponies. I think I know the one that will be yours while you're here."

"Yippee!" Until this moment Tracy hadn't thought her son's face would ever light up like that again.

"You can name her," he added.

Johnny looked perplexed. "I don't know any girl names for a horse."

"You think about it tonight, and tell me tomorrow."

"Okay."

Carson smiled at both of them before closing the door. She heard him cough again before he walked around the car and got in behind the wheel. Something he'd picked up after being deployed, he'd said.

"What makes you cough so much?"

He looked over at Johnny. "There were a lot of contaminants in the air in Afghanistan. Stuff like smoke and toxins. Some of the soldiers breathed too many bad fumes and our lungs were injured. When I got sick, I was sent to a hospital in Maryland for special treatment. That's where I met Ross and Buck. We became such good friends, we decided to go into business together after we got home."

"Oh. Does it hurt?" Johnny almost whispered the last word.

"It did in the beginning, but not so much now. We're a lot better than we used to be."

"I'm glad."

Her sweet boy.

"Me too, son."

War was a ghastly reality of life. Carson and his friends were some of the fortunate ones who came home alive. She admired them for getting on with living despite their problem, for unselfishly wanting to make a difference in her life and Johnny's. What generous, remarkable men....

As he drove them toward the town, she stared out the window. With night coming on, the Tetons formed a giant silhouette against the growing darkness. She shivered in reaction.

Instead of Johnny, who carried on an animated conversation with their host about horses and breeds, *she* was the one who felt oddly troubled for being so far away from home and everything familiar to her. This new world had taken her by surprise in ways she couldn't understand or explain.

Chapter Two

Carson pulled the van in front of the newly erected cabin designated for the Baretta family. He'd asked one of the girls from town who did housekeeping to keep the lights on after she left. Earlier he'd made certain there were snacks for the Barettas, and in the minifridge he'd stored plenty of juices and sodas.

It had grown quiet during the drive from Jackson to the ranch. When he looked in the rearview mirror, he saw Johnny was fast asleep. The cute little guy had finally conked out.

Carson got out and opened the rear door of the van. His gaze met Tracy's. He handed her the key. "If you'll open the door, I'll carry him inside."

She gathered the sacks with their purchases and hurried ahead of him. The front room consisted of a living room with a couch and chairs and a fireplace. On one wall was an entertainment center with a TV, DVD player and a supply of family movies for the guests. Against the other wall was a rectangular table and chairs. A coffeemaker and a microwave sat on one end near the minifridge.

The back hallway divided into two bedrooms and a bathroom. He swept past her to one of the bedrooms and deposited Johnny on one of the twin beds. He didn't weigh a lot. The boy was built like his father and had the brunette hair and brown eyes of his Italian ancestry.

He was Tony Baretta's son, all right. You wouldn't think he belonged to his blonde mother until you saw his facial features. Pure northern European, like hers. An appealing combination.

As for Tracy Baretta with her gray-green eyes, she was just plain appealing. Unexpectedly lovely. Womanly.

In the guys' desire to make this week memorable for their family, he simply hadn't counted on…*her.*

While she started taking off Johnny's shoes, Carson went back outside to bring in the luggage. "If you need anything, just pick up the phone and one of the staff will answer, day or night. Tomorrow morning, walk over to the main ranch house. We serve breakfast there from six to nine in the big dining room. Lunch is from twelve to two and dinner from five to eight.

"I'll watch for you and introduce you to the guys. They're anxious to meet you. After that, we'll plan your day. For your information, different sets of tourists are staying in the other cabins, but you're the only family here at our invitation for this coming week. In another month we're expecting our next family."

She followed him to the front door of the cabin. "Thank you for everything, Carson." Her voice cracked. "To be honest, I'm overwhelmed. You and your friends are so good to do what you're doing. I could never repay you for this." Tears glistened in her eyes. "From the time you met us at the airport, my son has been a different child. That picture meant everything to him."

To her, too, he wagered.

"Losing your husband has been a traumatic experience for you. My friends and I know that. Even though anyone in the military, and their family, is aware that death can come, no one's ready for it. When our division heard about Tony, we all suffered because he left a wife and child. We're like brothers out there. When one gets hurt, we all hurt."

She nodded. "Tony talked a lot about his buddies. He was so proud to serve with you."

"That goes both ways. There's no way we can bring him back to you, but we'd like to put a smile back on your son's face, if only for a little while. I promise that while you're here, we'll treat him with sensitivity and try to keep him as happy and safe as is humanly possible."

She smiled warmly. "I know you will." He could feel her sincerity.

"We have other guests coming to the ranch all the time, but you and Johnny are our special visitors. No one knows that we've nicknamed this place the Daddy Dude Ranch. What we hope to do is try to lend ourselves out as dads to take some of the burden off you."

Her hazel eyes glistened with tears. "You've already done that. Did you see Johnny in that shop earlier, walking around in those Western clothes with that huge smile on his face? He put that cowboy hat on just the way you wear yours and tried walking like you do in his new cowboy boots. I never saw anything so cute in my life."

"You're right about that." Carson thought he'd never seen anything so beautiful as the woman standing in front of him.

"That mustang we bought was like giving him a bag of Oreos with just the centers."

Carson chuckled. "He likes those?"

"He has a terrible sweet tooth."

"Didn't we all?"

"Probably. Let me say once again how honored I feel that you picked our family. It was a great thrill to receive your letter. Already I can tell Johnny is thriving on this kind of attention. What you're doing is inspirational."

From the light behind them, he could pick out gold and silver filaments in the hair she wore fastened at her nape. Opposites had attracted to produce Johnny. Carson was having trouble concentrating on their conversation.

"Thank you, Tracy. He's a terrific boy."

"For a man who's never had children, you're so good with him. Where did you learn those skills?"

"That's because my grandfather was the best and put up with me and my friends. If it rubbed off on me, then I'm glad."

"So am I. Johnny's having a marvelous time."

"I had a wonderful evening, too, believe me. If I didn't say it before, welcome to the Teton Valley Ranch. Now I'll wish you good-night."

He left quickly and headed for the van. It was a short drive to the main house where he'd been raised. He pulled in back and entered through the rear door. Ross was still in the den working on the accounts when Carson walked down the hall.

"Hey—" Ross called to him. "How did everything go with the Baretta family?"

"Hang on while I grab a cup of coffee and I'll tell you."

"I could use one, too. I'll come with you." They walked down another hall to the kitchen, both coughing up a storm en route.

"Where's Buck?"

"In town, getting some more materials to do repairs on the bunkhouse. He should have been back by now."

"Unless he made a stop at Bubba's Barbecue to see you-know-who."

"Since his last date with Nicole after she got off work, I don't think he's interested after all. She called here twice today. He didn't return the calls."

"Why am I not surprised?" Buck was a confirmed bachelor, as were they all.

Carson grabbed a donut. The cook, who lived in town, had gone home for the night. They had the kitchen to themselves. No sooner had he brewed a fresh pot of coffee than they heard Buck coughing before he appeared in the doorway.

In a minute the three of them filled their mugs and sat down at the old oak table where Carson had eaten most of the meals in his life with his grandparents. Until he'd gone into the Marines. But he didn't want to think about that right now. The guys wanted to know how things had gone at the airport.

"Johnny Baretta is the cutest little six-year-old you ever saw in your life." He filled them in on the details. "He swallowed a couple of bites of that buffalo burger like a man."

They smiled. "How about his mom?" Buck asked.

Carson took a long swig of his coffee. How to answer them... "Nice."

Ross burst into laughter. "That's it? Nice?"

No. That *wasn't* it. "When you meet her in the morning at breakfast, you can make your own assessment." He knew exactly how they'd react. "She's very grateful."

Both men eyed him with speculation. Buck drained his mug. "What's the plan for tomorrow?"

"After breakfast I'll take them over to the barn and give them a riding lesson. Later in the day I thought they'd appreciate a drive around the ranch to get their bearings, and we'll go from there. What about you?"

"I'm going to get the repairs done on the bunkhouse in the morning. Then I'll be taking the Holden party on an overnight campout. We'll be back the next day."

Ross got up from the table to wash their mugs. "The Harris party is planning to do some fly fishing. If Johnny wants to join us, come and find me."

"That boy is game for anything." Tony Baretta had been a lucky man in many ways. He shouldn't have been the one to get killed by a roadside bomb. Carson could still hear Johnny say, *I loved my dad.* The sound of the boy's broken heart would always haunt him.

He pushed himself away from the table, causing Buck to give him a second glance. "What's up?"

Carson grimaced. "When we thought up this idea, we hadn't met these people. It was pure hell to look into that little guy's eyes last night and see the sadness. I hadn't counted on caring so m—" Another coughing spell attacked him, preventing him from finishing his thought.

He needed his inhaler and headed for the hall. "I'll see you two in the morning." Ross would do a security check and lock up.

Carson had taken over his grandfather's room on the ground floor. The other two had bedrooms on the second floor. It was a temporary arrangement. At the end of the summer they'd assess their dude ranch experiment.

If they decided it wasn't working, either or both of them could still work on the ranch and make Wyoming their permanent home. He'd already told them they could build their own houses on the property.

Once he reached the bedroom, he inhaled his medication and then took a shower followed by a sleeping pill. Tonight he needed to be knocked out. His old friend "guilt" was back with a double punch. He couldn't make up to his grandfather for the years away, and no power on earth could bring Johnny's father back.

Carson must have been out of his mind to think a week on the ranch was going to make a dent in that boy's pain. He knew for sure Tracy was barely functioning, but she was a mother who'd do anything to help her child get on with living. She had that hidden strength women were famous for. He could only admire her and lament his lack of it.

After getting into bed, he lay back against the pillow with a troubled sigh. He realized it was too late to decide not to go through with the dude ranch idea for the fallen soldiers' families. He and the guys had put three months of hard labor into their project to get everything ready. The Barettas had already arrived and were now asleep in one of the new cabins.

They had their work cut out for them, but Carson was afraid they'd fall short of their desire to make a difference. In fact he was *terrified*.

THE NEXT MORNING Tracy pulled on a pair of jeans and a sage-colored cotton sweater. It had a crew neck and long sleeves. She'd done some shopping before this trip. If it got hot later in the day, she'd switch to a blouse. The cowboy boots she'd bought last evening felt strange and would take some getting used to.

After giving her hair a good brush, she fastened it at the nape with a tortoise-shell clip. Once she'd put on lotion and applied lipstick, a shade between coral and pink, she was ready for the day.

"Who's hungry for breakfast?" she asked, coming out of the bathroom into the sunny room with its yellow and white motif. But it was a silly question because Johnny didn't hear her. He'd been dressed for half an hour in his new duds, complete with a black cowboy hat and boots, and was busy loading his mustang again. Already he'd gone through a couple of rolls of caps, waking her up with a start.

She'd bought him three dozen rolls to keep him supplied, but at this rate he'd go through them by the end of the day. It was a good thing the cabins weren't too close together.

Tracy slipped the key in her pocket. "Come on, honey." She opened the door and immediately let out a gasp as she came face-to-face with the Grand Teton. In the morning sun it looked so different from last night when she'd had the sensation of it closing in on her. Against an impossibly blue sky, she'd never seen anything as glorious in her life.

Between the vista of mountains and the strong scent of sage filling the dry air, Tracy felt as if they'd been transported to another world. Even Johnny stopped fiddling with his cap gun to look. "Those sure are tall mountains!"

"They're magnificent!"

She locked the door and they started walking along the dirt road to the sprawling two-story ranch house in the distance. It was the kind you saw in pictures of the Old West, owned by some legendary cattle king.

"I hope they have cereal."

Tracy hoped they didn't. He needed to get off candy and sugar-coated cereal, his favorites when he could get away with it. His grandmother made all kinds of fabulous pasta, but he only liked boring mac and cheese out of the box. "Carson mentioned eggs, bacon and buckwheat pancakes."

"What's buckwheat?"

She smiled. "You'll have to ask him." The poor man had already answered a hundred questions last evening. She'd been surprised at his patience with her son.

Her eyes took in the tourist log cabins where she saw cars parked. Many of the outbuildings were farther away. Last night, Carson had pointed out the ranch manager's complex with homes and bunkhouses. He'd mentioned a shed for machinery and hay, a calving barn, horse barn and corrals, but it had been too dark to pick everything out. To Tracy the hundred-year-old ranch resembled a small city.

At least a dozen vehicles, from trucks, vans, and four-wheel-drives to a Jeep without a top and several cars, were parked at the rear of the ranch house. She kept walking with Johnny to the front, admiring the workmanship and the weathered timbers. The house had several decks, with a grove of trees to the side to provide shade. The first Lundgren knew what he was doing, to stake out his claim in this paradise.

They rounded the corner and walked up the steps to the entrance. An office was located to the left of the rustic foyer. At a glance to the right, the huge great room with a stone fireplace led into a big dining room with wagon-wheel chandeliers.

"Hi! Can I help you?"

Johnny walked over to the college-aged girl behind the counter. "Hi! We're waiting for Carson."

The friendly brunette leaned over to smile at him. "You must be Johnny Baretta from Ohio."

"Yup. What's your name?"

"Susan. Anything you need, you ask me. Mr. Lundgren told me to tell you to go right on through to the dining room and he'd meet you there."

"Thank you," Tracy spoke for both of them.

"Welcome to the ranch, Mrs. Baretta."

"We're thrilled to be here. Come on, honey."

They were almost to the dining room when a handsome, fit-looking man, probably Carson's age and height, came forward. Though he wore a plaid shirt and jeans, with his shorter cropped black hair she could imagine him in Marine gear. His brown eyes played over her with male interest before they lit on Johnny.

"I'm Ross Livingston, Carson's friend. You must be the brave guy who ate a buffalo burger last night."

"Well…" He looked at Tracy. "Not all of it," Johnny answered honestly. "It was too big."

"I know, and I'm impressed you got through most of it."

Tracy laughed and he joined her, provoking the same kind of cough she'd heard come out of Carson. "Excuse me," he said after it had subsided. "It's not contagious in case you were worried."

"We're not. Carson already explained."

"Good. He got detained on the phone, but he should

be here in a minute. Come into the dining room with me, Johnny, and we'll get you served."

They followed him. "Do you know if they have cereal?"

"Sure. What kind do you like?"

"Froot Loops."

"You're in luck."

"Goody!"

Tracy refrained from bursting his bubble. Tomorrow they'd choose something else.

Ross guided them across dark, vintage hardwood floors in keeping with the Western flavor to an empty table with a red-and-white-checked cloth. A vase of fresh white daisies had been placed on each table. She found this setting charming.

When he helped them to be seated, he took a chair and handed them Saturday's menu from the holder. "In a minute the waitress will come to take your order."

She scanned the menu.

"Mom? Do they have hot chocolate?"

Tracy couldn't lie. "Yes."

"Then that's what I want with my cereal."

"I'll let you have it if you'll eat some meat. There's sausage, bacon or ham."

"And brook trout," Ross interjected, smiling into her eyes as he said it.

She chuckled. "I think after the buffalo burger, we'll hold off on the fish for another day."

As he broke into laughter, the waitress came to the table, but she hadn't come alone. Their host had arrived without his hat, wearing another Western shirt in a tan color. The chiseled angles of his hard-boned features drew her gaze for the second time in twelve hours. He was all male.

"Carson!"

"Hey, partner—" He sat down next to Ross and made the introductions.

"Where's your hat?"

"I'll put it on after breakfast."

"I want to keep mine on."

"Except that it might be hard to eat with it," Tracy declared. "Let me put it on the empty chair until after."

"Okay."

The waitress took their orders and left.

Ross got up from the table. "Hey, Johnny, while you're waiting for your food, I'll take you out to the foyer and show you something amazing before I leave. Since I've already eaten, I have a group of guests waiting for me to take them fishing."

"What is it?" Ross had aroused his curiosity.

"Come with me and see."

"I'll be right back, Mom."

"Okay."

As they walked away, she heard Ross say, "I'm glad you came, Johnny. We're going to have a lot of fun while you and your mom are here."

"Your friend is nice," Tracy told Carson.

He studied her features for a moment, seeming to reflect on what she'd said. "He's the best. Right now he's showing Johnny the big moose head that was mounted years before I was born. It's the granddaddy of them all, but you don't see it until you're leaving to go outside."

"He's fascinated by the big animals."

"Did your husband hunt, or any of your family?"

"No."

"I've never been much of a hunter, either, but my grandfather allowed licensed hunters to use the land during the hunting season, so I do, too. I much prefer to see the elk and deer alive. There's great opportunity here to photograph the animals. I'll show Johnny lots of spots. He can hide in the trees and take pictures of squirrels and rabbits, all the cute little forest creatures."

"He'll go crazy."

"That's the idea."

To her consternation, Tracy found herself studying his rugged features and looked away. "There's so much to do here, it's hard to know where to start. When I read your brochure on the internet, I couldn't believe it."

He had an amazing white smile. "Most people can't do it all. They find something they love and stick to it. That'll be the trick with Johnny. We'll try him out on several things and see what he likes most."

"Mom—" He came running back into the dining room, bringing her back to the present. "You've got to see this moose! It's humongous!" That was Cory's favorite word.

"I promise I'll get a look at it when we go outside."

"Its head is as big as the Pierce's minicar!"

Carson threw back his head and laughed so hard, everyone in the room looked over. As for Tracy, she felt his rich male belly laugh clear through her stomach to her toes. The laugh set off another of his coughing spells. His blue eyes zeroed in on her. "Who are the Pierces?"

"Our neighbors down the street in Sandusky."

Johnny sat back down. "Ross thinks he looks like a supersize Bullwinkle."

"He's that, all right."

Tracy smiled at him. "I have a feeling you and Ross

are both big teases. Can I presume your other friend is just as bad?"

"He has his moments," he drawled. "You'll meet Buck tomorrow when he's back from taking some guests on an overnight campout."

"Can we go on one of those?"

Carson's brilliant blue gaze switched to Johnny. "I'm planning on it."

Johnny's face lit up. "I want to see that elk with the giant antlers."

"You liked that picture?"

"Yeah. It was awesome."

"I couldn't agree more, but I don't know if he's still around. My grandpa took that picture a few years ago. Tell you what. When we're out driving and hiking, we'll look for him."

The waitress came with their food. Tracy's omelet was superb. She ate all of it and was gratified to see Johnny finish his ham. Carson put away steak and eggs, then got up from the table.

"Give me five minutes and I'll meet you out in front in the Jeep. We'll drive over to the barn." He coughed for a moment. "Normally we'd walk, but I'm planning to give you a tour of the property after your riding lesson. It'll save time. The restrooms are down the hall from the front desk."

"Thank you. The breakfast was delicious by the way."

"I'm glad you enjoyed it." He turned to leave.

"See you in a minute, Carson! Don't forget your hat!"

That kid made him chuckle. He'd done a lot of it since last evening. More than he'd done in a long time.

He walked through the doors to the kitchen and nodded to the staff. After putting some bottled water and half a dozen oranges and plums in a bag, he headed down another hall to the bedroom for his Stetson.

Making certain he had his cell on him, he headed out the rear door of the ranch with more energy than usual. Susan would phone him if there were any problems. After stashing the bag in the backseat, he started the engine and took off.

Try as he might, when he drove around the gravel drive to the front, he couldn't take his eyes off Tracy Baretta. From the length of her sinuous body to her blond hair gleaming in the morning sun, she was a knockout. But she didn't seem to know it. That was part of her attraction.

"There's nothing wrong with looking," his grandfather used to say to him. "But if a woman's off-limits, then that's the way you keep it." Carson had adopted that motto and it had kept him out of a hell of a lot of trouble.

This woman was Tony Baretta's widow and still grieving for him.

Shut it off, Lundgren.

Johnny started toward him. "Can I ride in front with you?"

"You bet." He jumped out and went around to open both doors for them, trying to take his own advice as he helped Tracy into the backseat.

Once they got going, Johnny let out a whoop of excitement. "I've never ridden in a Jeep before. This is more fun than riding on a fire engine."

"I don't believe it."

"It's true!"

Carson glanced at him. "I've never been on one."

"If you come back to Ohio, my uncles will let you go on their ladder truck."

"Sounds pretty exciting. But wait till you ride a horse. You'll love it so much, you won't want to do anything else."

"What's your horse's name?"

"I've had a lot of them. My latest one is a gelding named Blueberry. He's a blue roan."

Johnny giggled. "You have a blue horse?"

"Seeing's believing. Wait till you meet your palomino. She's a creamy gold color with a white mane and tail." *Almost as beautiful as your mother.* "Have you thought of a name yet?"

"No."

"That's okay. It'll come to you."

They headed for the barn. He'd talked to Bert ahead of time. The pony had been put in the corral so Johnny would see it first off. He drove the Jeep around till they came to the entrance to the corral. There stood the pony in the sun. Carson stopped the Jeep.

"Oh, Johnny—look at that adorable pony!"

The boy stared for the longest time before scrambling out of the front seat. He'd left his mustang behind.

"Wait!" His mother hurried after him, but he'd already reached the fencing before she caught up to him.

Carson joined them. "Isn't she a little beauty?"

Johnny's head jerked toward him. The excitement on his face was worth a thousand words. "I'm going to call her Goldie."

"That's the perfect name for her." The pony walked right over to them. "Good morning, Goldie. This is Johnny. He's flown a long way to meet you."

Carson lifted the boy so he could reach over the

railing. "You notice that pretty white marking? That's her forelock. Watch what happens when I rub it. She's gentle and likes being touched."

The pony nickered and nudged closer. "See?"

Johnny giggled and carefully put out his hand to imitate Carson's gesture. He got the same reaction from Goldie who moved her head up and down, nickering more intensely this time.

"She loves it and wants you to do it some more."

As he patted the horse with increasing confidence, Tracy flashed Carson a smile. It came from her eyes as well as her mouth. That was a first.

He dragged his glance away with reluctance. "Come into the barn with me, Johnny. We'll go in the tack room to pick out her saddle."

"Tack room?"

Carson shared another smile with Tracy. "It's a room where we keep the saddles and bridles for the horses."

"Oh." Johnny jumped down. "We'll be right back, Mom."

Carson had a hunch the boy was hooked. You never knew. Some kids showed little interest or were too scared and didn't want to ride. This little guy was tough. *Like his father.*

"I'll be waiting."

Johnny asked a dozen questions while they gathered everything, impressing Carson with his bright mind that wanted to learn. This was a new world for Carson who, as an adult, had never spent time taking care of anyone's child. He found Johnny totally entertaining and quite wonderful.

As a kid, Carson had grown up around the children whose parents worked on the ranch, and of course, the neighbor's kids. A couple of the boys, including his best friend Jean-Paul, wanted to be rodeo champions. So did Carson, whose grandfather had been a champion and taught him everything he knew.

In between chores and school, they'd spent their free time on the back of a horse, learning how to be bull-doggers and bull riders. As they grew older there were girls, and later on women, prize money and championships. But it still wasn't enough. He'd wanted to get out and see the world. He'd joined the Marines on a whim, wanting a new arena.

Through it all, Carson had taken and taken, never giving anything back. The pain over his own selfishness would never go away, but Johnny's enthusiasm wouldn't allow him time to wallow in it.

He carried the equipment to the corral and put the bridle on Goldie. Johnny stood by him, watching in fascination. "Here you go. Hold the reins while I get her saddled."

The pony moved forward and nudged Johnny. He laughed and was probably scared to death, but he held on. "She likes you or she wouldn't do that. You'll get used to it."

Carson threw on the blanket, then the saddle. "Okay. Now I'd like you to walk around the corral leading Goldie. Just walk normally, holding on to the reins. She'll follow. It will help her to learn to trust you, because she's nervous. Do you want me to walk with you, or do you want to do it yourself?"

He thought for a minute. "I can do it."

"Fine."

The whole time this went on, Carson was aware of his mother watching in silence from the fence as her brave son did a slow walk around the enclosure without a misstep. At one point she took some pictures with her cell phone.

"Great job, Johnny. Now walk her to that feeding bag. Dig in and pull out a handful of oats. If you hold them out to her with your hand flat, she'll eat them without hurting you, but it'll tickle."

Johnny laughed nervously, but he did what Carson told him to do. In a minute he was giggling while the pony enjoyed her treat. "It feels funny." He heard Tracy laugh from the sidelines.

"You've made a friend for life, Johnny. Think you're ready to get up on her?" The boy nodded. "Okay." Now the next lesson was about to begin. "I'm going to seat you in the saddle, then I'll adjust the stirrups." Carson lifted him. "You hold on to the reins and the pommel. Are you all right? I know it seems a long way up. Did you ever fall off the tricky bars at school?"

"Yes."

"Well, this is a lot safer because you've got this pony under you and she loves you. She doesn't want you to fall. Okay if I let go of you?"

"Okay," he said in a shaky voice.

Carson took a few steps back, ready to catch him if he suddenly wanted to get off. But he didn't. "Good man."

"You look like a real cowboy!" his mother called out. "I'm so proud of you!"

"Thanks."

Moving to the front of the pony Carson said, "I'm going to take hold of the bridle and walk Goldie. You keep holding on to the pommel so you can feel what it's like to ride her. Does that sound okay to you?"

Johnny nodded, but was biting his lip.

"We'll only go a few feet, then we'll stop."

"Okay," the boy murmured.

Carson started to walk. Goldie cooperated. When he stopped, she stopped. "How did that feel? Do you want to keep going?"

"Yes."

"Good for you. I've seen ten-year-olds out here who started bawling their heads off for their moms about now." He moved again and just kept going until they'd circled the corral. "You just passed your first lesson with flying colors, Johnny." He heard clapping and cheers from Tracy.

A big smile broke out on his face. "Thanks. Can I go around by myself now?"

That's what he'd been hoping to hear, but you never knew. "Why not? Let me show you how to hold the reins. If she goes too fast, just pull back on them a little. Ready?" He nodded.

"I'm going to give Goldie a little tap on her hind quarters to get her going. Okay?"

"Yup."

Suddenly they were off at the same speed as before, but without his help. Carson walked over to the fence where Tracy was hanging over it.

"Hey—I'm doing it. I'm riding!" he cried out.

"You sure are," she called back. "I can't believe it!"

"It's easy, Mom." He circled one more time. "Now it's your turn."

Carson saw the expression on her face and chuckled. "Yeah, Mom. It's easy. Now it's time for you. Better not let your son show you up."

"He already has. I'm quaking in my new leather boots."

"I shivered my first time, too, but I promise it will be okay. Annie's a gentle, sure-footed mare."

She got down off the fence and walked around to enter the corral. Carson waited until Goldie had come up to him before he removed the boy's feet from the stirrups and pulled him off. "Give her a rub on the forelock, then she'll know you had a good time."

Johnny did his bidding without any hesitation. "Can I give her some more oats?"

"Of course." He handed him the reins. "Go ahead. You know what to do."

While he walked her over to the feed bag, Carson called to Bert to bring out Annie, and then he made the introductions. "Bert Rawlins, this is Tracy Baretta. Bert has been running the stable for years."

Tracy shook his hand. "It's a pleasure to meet you."

"The feeling's mutual, ma'am. Annie's saddled and ready to go."

Carson reached for the reins and handed them to Tracy. "Let's see how good a teacher I am."

There was more green than gray in her eyes today. They were suspiciously bright. "You already know. My son's over there feeding that pony like he's been living on this ranch for a month."

Nothing could have pleased Carson more. He watched her move in front of the bay and rub her forelock. She nickered on cue.

"This is my first time, Annie. Don't let me down." Pulling on the reins, she started walking around the corral just as her son had done.

Carson decided the brown horse with the black mane

and tail provided the perfect foil for her gleaming blond hair. When she came around, he helped her into the saddle and adjusted her stirrups. "Would you like me to walk you around?"

"I think I'll be all right." What did they say about a mother walking into a burning building for her child?

He handed her the reins and gave the horse's rump a tap. Annie knew what to do and started walking. Halfway around the arena, Carson knew Tracy would be all right.

"Hey, Mom—it's fun, huh?"

"It will be when I've had a few more lessons."

Annie kept walking toward Carson. He looked up at Tracy. "Want to go around one more time, pulling on the reins to the right or left?"

"Sure."

He was sure she didn't, but she was game.

"This time, give her a nudge with your heels and she'll go."

The second she made contact, Annie started out. It surprised Tracy, knocking her off balance, but she righted herself in a hurry.

"If she's going too fast, pull on the reins and she'll slow down."

Little by little she made it around the enclosure, urging the horse in one direction, then another.

"You're doing great, Mom!"

"You both are. I think that will be all for today."

Carson signaled Bert to take care of the horses. "Come on, Johnny." He walked over to help Tracy, but she was too quick for him. She flung her leg over and got down on her own. Whether she did it without thinking or didn't want help, he didn't know.

"Are we going for a Jeep ride now?"

"Would you like that, partner?"

"Yes. Then can we come back to see Goldie? I think she'll miss me."

Johnny was showing the first signs of a horse lover. Either it was in you, or it wasn't. "I'm sure she will."

The three of them got back in the Jeep. For the next hour, he gave them a tour of the property so they could get their bearings. Johnny talked up a storm while a quieter Tracy sat back and took in the sights. As they neared the ranch house, his cell phone rang. The caller ID indicated it was the district ranger for the Bridger-Teton National Forest.

"Excuse me for a minute. I have to take this," he said to them before answering. "Dave? What's up?"

"There's a man-made fire started up on the western edge of the forest bordering your property."

Carson grimaced. Tourist season always brought on a slew of forest fires.

"I've assembled two crews and am asking for any volunteers who can help stamp it out to meet up at the shadow rock trailhead," Dave continued. "There's not much wind. I think we can contain it before it spreads."

Before hanging up, Carson said, "I'll rustle up as many of the hands as I can and we'll be there shortly."

This would happen today, of all days. The hell of it was, with his disease, he didn't dare help fight the fire. Smoke was his enemy. All he could do was bring help and wear his oxygen apparatus.

Johnny looked at him. "Do you think I can take another ride on Goldie after dinner? I want to turn her in different directions and do stuff with her."

"I suppose that's up to your mother." Carson's gaze flicked to Tracy. "Did you hear that, Mom? What do you say?"

Chapter Three

Tracy heard it. In fact, she heard and saw so many things already, she was starting to experience turmoil. Johnny was eating up all the attention Carson showered on him. It would continue nonstop until next Saturday when they flew home.

With all their own family and work responsibilities, none of Johnny's uncles could give him this kind of time. Not even Tony had spent every waking hour with their son in the due course of a day. No father did, unless they were on vacation. Even then there were other distractions.

Few fathers had the skills or showed the infinite patience of this ex-marine rancher who seemed to be going above and beyond any expectations. He had to be a dream come true for her son, who'd been emotionally starving for a male role model since Tony's death.

When she'd accepted the invitation to come to the ranch, she hadn't realized these former soldiers would spend their own personal time this way. She had assumed the ranch staff would offer activities to entertain them. Period.

This was different.
Carson was different.

By giving Johnny that photo of his father, Carson had formed a bond with her son that wasn't going to go away. Carson might not see what was happening, but every moment invested for Johnny's sake increased her son's interest.

Tracy couldn't allow that to happen. Before long they'd be leaving this place, never to return. Johnny was still dealing with his father's death. They didn't need another crisis after they got home. She had to do something quickly to fix things before he got too attached to this incredible man. Tracy had to acknowledge that, so far, he *was* incredible, which was exactly what made her so uneasy.

While he'd driven them around the breathtaking property, giving them fruit and water, she'd sat in the back of the Jeep planning what she would say to Carson when she could get him alone. Another lesson at the corral after dinner was not an option.

Tonight after they'd eaten, she and Johnny would watch a movie in their cabin until he fell asleep. Then she'd phone Carson and have an important talk with him. Once he understood her concerns, he would make certain his partners spent equal time with Johnny. By the time he pulled up in front of their cabin to let them out, she felt more relaxed about her decision.

"I kept you longer than planned, but we're still in time for lunch."

Johnny looked up at him. "What are you going to have, Carson?"

"I think a grilled cheese sandwich and a salad."

"Me, too."

Since when? Tracy mused.

Carson tipped his Stetson. "See you two inside."

She slid out, not wanting to analyze why what he just did gave her a strange feeling in her tummy, as Johnny was wont to say. "Come on, honey. Don't forget your mustang."

To her relief, Carson drove off. "Let's use the restroom first, then maybe we'll find some other kids and you can play with them."

A few minutes later they entered the dining room. Ross was seated at a larger table with some tourists, including a couple of children. He waved her over. "Come and sit with us, Tracy. We're all going to do some more fishing after we eat and hope you'll join us."

Bless you, Ross.

"Johnny? Meet Sam Harris, who's seven, and Rachel Harris, who's nine. They're from Florida. This is Johnny Baretta from Ohio. He's six."

"I'm almost seven!"

Tracy smiled. "That's true. Your birthday is in a month." He'd be one of the older ones in his class in the fall.

After they sat down, Ross finished introducing her to Monica and Ralph Harris, who were marine biologists. The Tetons had to be a complete change of scenery for them, too.

Soon the waitress came over and took everyone's order. Carson still hadn't come. Tracy knew Johnny was looking for him.

Sam, the towheaded boy, glanced at Johnny. "How long are you here for?"

"A week."

"Same here. Then our parents have to get back to work."

"Oh."

"Where's your dad?" Rachel asked.

Johnny had faced this question many times, but Tracy knew it was always painful for him. "He died in the war."

"That's too bad," she said, sounding genuinely sad. "Do you like to fish?"

"My dad took me a couple of times."

"We'll catch our limit this afternoon," Ross chimed in, no doubt anxious to change the topic of conversation.

By the time lunch arrived, Carson had come into the dining room and walked over to their table, but he didn't sit down. Ross introduced him to everyone while they ate. "Mr. Lundgren's great-great-grandfather purchased this land in 1908 and made it into the Teton Valley Ranch."

"The ranch house was a lot smaller than this in the beginning," Carson informed them.

"You're sure lucky to live here," Sam uttered.

"We're lucky you came to visit."

Carson always knew the right thing to say to make everyone feel good.

"To my regret, something's come up and I won't be able to join you this afternoon, but Ross is an expert and will show all of you where to catch the biggest fish. When you bring them in, we'll ask the cook to fix them for your dinner. There's no better-tasting trout than a German brown."

"He ought to know," Ross interjected. "He was fishing the Snake with his grandpa when he was just a toddler."

Everyone laughed except Johnny, who'd become exceptionally quiet.

"Enjoy your day. See you later," Carson said. His

glance included Tracy and Johnny before he hurried out of the dining room.

"Where's he going?" her son whispered.

"I don't know, honey." Something had come up. Though he'd shown nothing tangible, she'd felt his tension. "He runs this ranch with his friends and has a lot of other things to do." *Thank heaven.*

"Do we have to go fishing?" He'd only eaten half of his grilled cheese and didn't touch the green salad, which was no surprise.

"Yes." Her automatic instinct had been to say no, because she was afraid to push him too hard. But right now she decided to take the psychologist's advice and practice a little tough love. "It'll be fun for both of us. I've never been fly fishing and want to try it."

"Okay," he finally muttered. At least he hadn't fought her on it. "But I bet I don't catch one."

"I bet you do. Think how fun it will be to phone your grandparents tonight and tell them everything."

This was the way their vacation was supposed to be. Doing all sorts of activities with different people. Unfortunately, Carson had gotten there first and had spoiled her son. Nothing and no one was more exciting than he was, even Tracy recognized that.

Ross got up from the table. "I'll bring the van in front and we'll go." He came around to her side. "Is everything all right?" He'd assumed there'd been a hard moment at the table for Johnny. He'd assumed correctly, but for the wrong reason. She couldn't tell Ross what was really going on inside Johnny, not when these wonderful marines were doing everything in their power to bring her son some happiness.

She smiled at him. For once this wasn't about Tony,

or Johnny's sensitivity to a child's question. This was about Carson. "Everything's fine. Honestly. See you in a minute."

Sam got out of his chair and came over to Johnny, who was putting another roll of caps into his mustang. "Where did you get that cap gun?"

"In Jackson. Carson took us."

He turned to his parents. "Can we go into town and buy one?"

"I want one, too," Rachel chimed in.

Their mother gave Tracy that "what are you going to do?" look. Tracy liked her. "Maybe after we're through fishing."

Tracy took her son aside. "Why don't you go out front and let them shoot your gun for a minute?"

"Do I have to?"

"No, but it's a good way to make friends, don't you think?"

A big sigh escaped. "I guess." He turned to Sam. "Do you guys want to try shooting some caps outside?"

"Heck, yes!"

They both ran out and Rachel followed. Tracy walked over to the parents who thanked her.

"I'm glad Johnny has someone to play with. After dinner we could all drive into town and take you to the Boot Corral. You can get a cap gun and cowboy hats there, in fact, everything Western."

"That's a wonderful idea!"

"I'm afraid my son would sleep in all his gear and new cowboy boots if I let him."

Both Harrises grinned as they headed out of the dining room for the foyer. "This is a fabulous place," Ralph commented. "I wish we could stay a month."

Tracy understood how he felt. She was grateful his children would be here for Johnny. If she could drum up enough activities that included them until they flew home, maybe a talk with Carson wasn't necessary. She needed to let things play out naturally before she got paranoid. No doubt other families with children would be staying here, too, and her worries would go away.

The next time Johnny brought up Carson's name, she'd impress upon him that the owner of the ranch had too many responsibilities to be on hand all hours of the day.

Unfortunately, his name surfaced after their wonderful trout dinner when they'd all decided to go into town and do some shopping.

"I don't want to go, Mom. Carson's going to give me another lesson on Goldie."

"But he's not here, honey. We'll have to wait until tomorrow. Tell you what. After we get back from town, you and the kids can go swimming. How does that sound?"

He thought about it for a minute before he said, "Okay." Convincing him was like pulling teeth, but he liked the Harris children well enough to give in.

As it turned out, once they were back from town loaded with hats, guns and more ammo than they could use in a week, they realized it was too cool outside to swim. Monica suggested they play Ping-Pong in the game room off the dining room.

Tracy agreed and told Johnny to go along with them. She'd come back to the ranch house as soon as she'd freshened up. When she walked in the bedroom for their jackets, her cell phone rang. She checked the caller ID. It had to be her mother-in-law calling.

"Hello, Sylvia?"

"No, it's Natalie. We came over for dinner before we leave on our trip in the morning. I'm using her phone to call because I can't find mine. How are you doing by now? Or, more to the point, how's Giovanni? Is he begging to go back home? I've wondered how he would handle things. I guess you realize our father-in-law is worried about him."

That was no news. Since Tony's death, his father had tried to step in as father and grandfather.

"If you want to know the truth, things are going so well it's got me scared."

"What do you mean?"

"Mr. Lundgren might be a former marine, but he's the owner of this ranch and is this amazing cowboy who's showing Johnny the time of his life. My son has a new hero."

"Already?"

"I'm afraid so. You wouldn't recognize him."

"Why afraid?"

"That was a wrong choice of words."

"I don't think so. How old is this guy?"

Natalie always got to the crux. "Maybe twenty-nine, thirty. I don't know."

"Is he a hunk?"

"Nat—"

"He *is!*"

"Listen. I'd love to talk more, but I don't have time. This nice couple with two children is watching out for Johnny in the game room and he's waiting for me."

"You mean he's playing on his own without *you?*"

"I know that sounds unbelievable. In a nutshell, he's

had his first horseback ride on the most beautiful golden pony you've ever seen, and he's in love with her."

"Her?"

"He named her Goldie. You should see him riding around in the saddle like a pro, all decked out in Western gear and a cowboy hat. We'll bring the same outfit home for Cory."

"You actually got him over his fear long enough to ride a horse?" She sounded incredulous. Tracy understood. Since Tony's death, Johnny showed reluctance to try anything new.

"Mr. Lundgren gave him his first lesson."

"How did he accomplish that?"

Tracy told her about the photo of his father Carson had given him at the airport. "That was the magic connection that built his trust."

"You're right. He sounds like some wonderful guy. What's his wife like?"

Tracy gripped the phone tighter. "He's not married. Now, I really have to go. Have a great time on your trip to New York. We'll talk when I get back. Give our love to the family. *Ciao,* Nat."

There were no words to describe the ex-marine that would do him justice, so it was better not to try. No sooner had she disconnected than the phone on the bedside table started ringing. She assumed it was the front desk calling. Maybe it was Monica. She picked up. "Hello?"

"Hi, Tracy. It's Carson. Am I disturbing you?"

His deep voice rumbled through her. She sank down on her twin bed. After discussing him with Natalie, she needed the support. "Not at all. I was just on my way over to the ranch house to play Ping-Pong with the others."

"That sounds fun," he said before he started coughing. "I'm sorry about today. I'd fully intended to take you fishing and give Johnny another horseback riding lesson."

She gripped the phone a little tighter. "Please don't worry about that. Ross did the honors. Even *I* caught a twelve-incher. It was my first time fly fishing. I must admit it was a real thrill to feel that tug and reel it in."

"How did it taste?"

"Absolutely delicious."

"That's good," he murmured before coughing again.

She moistened her lips nervously for no good reason. "I take it you had to deal with an emergency."

"You could say that. A couple of college kids out backpacking in the forest didn't do a good enough job of putting out their campfire. It took several crews of rangers and forest service workers to keep it from spreading too far onto ranch property."

Her breath caught. That was why she'd felt his tension at the table. "How much did it burn?"

"Only a few acres this time."

"*This* time?"

"It happens every year." Suddenly he was hacking again. "Some fires are more devastating than others."

"Does that mean you were breathing smoke all day?"

"No. I rounded up the hands and drove them to the fire in shifts, but I took oxygen with me."

"Even so, you shouldn't have been near there with your problem," she said before she realized her voice was shaking.

"There was no one else to do the job. Undeserving as I am, I have to try to save what my grandfather willed to me."

She got to her feet. "What do you mean by undeserving?"

"Forget my ramblings. It slipped out by accident."

"And I heard it, which means you inhaled too much smoke today and don't feel well. You ought to be in bed."

"A good night's sleep is all I need. I'll let you go so you can join your son. It would be better not to tell him about the fire."

"Agreed." She couldn't let him hang up yet. "Carson, how long were you in the hospital?"

"About five weeks. From the end of January to the beginning of March."

"Were you all suffering from the same illness?"

"On our ward, yes."

His cough worried her. "Are you getting better?"

"We're certainly better than we were when we were flown in."

"I mean, are you going to get well?"

"We don't know."

She frowned. "You mean the doctor can't tell you?"

"Not really. They're doing studies on us. The day before we left the hospital, a general came to talk to us about asking Congress for the funding to help our cause."

"The Congress doesn't do enough," she muttered.

"Well, at least he came to our floor and said he's rooting for us, so that's better than nothing."

"Then you could have a lifelong ailment."

"That's right, but we can live with it, even if no one

else can. The ranch house gets pretty noisy when the three of us have a coughing fit together."

He tried to make light of it, but she wasn't laughing. "You're very brave."

"If you want to talk brave, let's talk about your husband. Why did he join the Marines?"

"His best friend went into the military and got killed by friendly gunfire. It tore Tony apart. He decided to join up to finish what his friend had started. We were already married, but I could tell he wanted it more than anything. We were lucky to go to Japan together before he was deployed to Afghanistan. It doesn't happen often that a marine can go there with his wife."

"You're right."

"During 9/11 I saw those firefighters run into those torched buildings and I wondered how they did it. Then I met Tony and understood. It's in his genes, I guess."

"Those genes saved lives, Tracy. That's why you can't talk about him in the same breath you talk about me and the guys. We're no heroes."

But they were.

"You shouldn't have gone near that fire today."

"That's the second time you've said it."

"I'm sorry. Johnny's been worried about you, too."

"Tracy," he said in a deep voice, "I appreciate your concern more than you know. I haven't had anyone worry about me in a long time. Thanks for caring. We'll see each other at breakfast. Good night."

He hung up too fast for her to wish him the same. Afraid he'd be up all night coughing, she knew that if she didn't hurry to the game room she'd brood over his condition. And his state of mind, which was none of her business and shouldn't be her concern. But to her chagrin, she couldn't think about anything else on her way to the ranch house.

CARSON HAD MEDICATED himself before going to bed, but he woke up late Sunday morning feeling only slightly better. It wasn't just his physical condition due to the smoke he'd inhaled the day before, despite the oxygen. When he'd phoned Tracy last night, he hadn't realized how vulnerable he'd been at the time. His sickness had worn him down and caused him to reveal a little of his inner turmoil, something he regretted.

She was a guest on the ranch. He was supposed to be helping to lift her burden for the week instead of talking about himself.

He grabbed his cell phone to call his ranch foreman and get an update on the progress with the fencing in the upper pasture. After they chatted for a few minutes, he dragged his body out of bed to shower and shave.

Once dressed, he walked through the ranch house to the kitchen and poured himself some coffee. He talked to the cook and kitchen help while he drank it, then entered the dining room and discovered a few guests still eating, but no sign of Tracy or Johnny. Ross would know what was going on.

Carson went to the office, but the place was empty. Since Buck wouldn't be back until lunchtime, he headed for the foyer to talk to Susan. "How's everything going?"

"Great!"

"Have you seen Ross?"

"Yes. Another couple of groups went fishing with him. Did you know that by this evening we'll be all booked up?"

"That's the kind of news I like to hear."

Like most ranches, the cattle operation on the Teton Valley Ranch had little, if any, margin. But the value of the land kept rising faster than the liability from raising cattle. It was either sell the hay, grass and cows to someone else, or borrow on the land when the market was down. In time he hoped the dude ranch idea would bring in its own source of revenue.

"Johnny Baretta was asking about you this morning. He can't wait for another horseback riding lesson."

That news pleased him even more. "Do you have any idea where he and his mother might be?"

"I heard him and the Harris children talking about going swimming. You should have seen how cute they all looked in their cowboy outfits when they came in for breakfast."

"I can imagine. Talk to you later."

He walked outside and headed around the other side of the house to the pool area. The swimming pool had been Buck's idea and was a real winner for children and people who simply wanted to laze about. The kids' shouts of laughter reached his ears before he came upon the two families enjoying the water.

"Carson!"

Johnny's shriek of excitement took him by surprise and touched him. "Hey, partner."

The boy scrambled out of the pool and came running over to him. Above his dark, wet hair he saw Tracy's silvery-gold head as she trod water. Their eyes met for a brief moment, causing a totally foreign adrenaline rush. "Can we go horseback riding now?"

"That's the plan," he said before breaking the eye contact.

Like clockwork, the other two children hurried over to him dripping water. "Will you take us riding, too?"

He chuckled. It brought on another coughing spell. "Of course. Anyone who wants a lesson, meet me at the corral in fifteen minutes!" he called out so the parents would hear him. They waved back in acknowledgment. As he turned to leave, he heard Rachel ask Johnny why Carson coughed so much.

"Because he breathed all this bad stuff in the war."

"What kind of stuff?" Sam wanted to know.

"Smoke and other junk."

"Ew. I hope I never have to go."

"I wish my dad had never joined the Marines." Johnny's mournful comment tore Carson apart.

He hurried back inside the ranch house to grab a bite of breakfast in the kitchen. While he downed bacon and eggs, he phoned Bert and asked him to start saddling Goldie and two of the other ponies.

After they hung up, he packed some food and drinks in a basket. In a minute, he left through the back door and placed the basket in the back of the truck, then climbed in. The interior still smelled of acrid smoke.

If the kids wanted some fun after their lesson, he'd let them get in the back and he'd drive them to the pasture to see the cattle. When he'd been a boy, he'd enjoyed walking around the new calves and figured they would, too.

When he reached the barn, he saddled Annie, but held off getting more horses ready for the Harrises. They might not want to ride, only watch their children.

Another lesson for Tracy and her son ought to be enough for them to take a short ride down by the Snake

River tomorrow. With enough practice, they'd be able to enjoy half-day rides around the property.

If Johnny could handle it, they'd camp out in the Bridger-Teton forest where there were breathtaking vistas of the surrounding country. Even if the journey would be bittersweet, he longed to show them his favorite places. Since joining the Marines, he hadn't done any of this.

Once Annie's bridle was on, he grasped the reins and walked her outside to the corral where Bert had assembled the ponies. In the distance, he saw the children running along the dirt road toward them. All three were dressed in their cowboy outfits.

Johnny reached him first. "Do you think Goldie missed me?"

"Why don't you give her forelock a rub and find out?"

Without hesitation he approached the golden palomino. "Hi, Goldie. It's me." He reached out to touch her. The pony nickered and nudged him affectionately. "Hey—" He turned to Carson. "Did you see that? She really likes me!"

While Burt grinned, Carson burst into laughter. It ended in a coughing spasm, but he didn't care. "She sure does."

"I'm going to feed her some oats." Seizing the reins without fear, he walked her over to the feed bag.

Knowing Bert would keep an eye on him, Carson approached the fence. Beneath the brim of his Stetson, his gaze fell on Tracy whose damp hair was caught back with a hair band. This morning she wore a tangerine-colored knit top and jeans her beautiful figure did amazing things for. "Are you ready for your next lesson?"

"I think so." Her smoky green eyes smiled at him before she entered the corral.

"Would you like some help mounting?"

"Thank you, but I'd like to see if I can do this on my own first."

This was the second time she hadn't wanted him to get too close. The first time he might have imagined it, but the second time led him to believe she was avoiding contact. He forced himself to look at the Harrises, who'd just come walking up.

"Should I ask Bert to saddle some horses for you?"

They shook their heads. Ralph leaned over the fence. "We've been riding before. Right now, we just want to see how the kids do."

"Understood." He turned to Johnny. "Hey, partner— why don't you help me show Rachel and Sam what you do before you get on."

"Sure! Which pony do you guys want?"

"That was a good question to ask them, Johnny."

Sam cried, "Can I have the brown one with the black tail?"

"Bruno is a great choice."

"I like the one with the little ears and big eyes. It's so cute."

Carson nodded. "That dappled gray filly is all yours, Rachel. Her name is Mitzi."

The children loved the names.

"Okay, Johnny. What do they do now?"

"They have to rub their noses so the ponies will know they like them."

The next few minutes were pure revelation as Tracy's son took the kids through the drill, step by step, until they were ready to mount.

Ridiculous as it was, Carson felt a tug on his emotions because Johnny had learned his lesson so quickly and was being such a perfect riding instructor. He glanced at Tracy several times. Without her saying anything, he knew she was bursting with motherly pride.

Soon all four of them were astride their horses. They circled the corral several times and played Follow the Leader in figure eights, Johnny's idea. Carson lounged against the fence next to the Harrises, entertained by the children who appeared to be having a terrific time. Since Tracy rode with them, Carson had a legitimate reason to study her without seeming obvious.

He threw out a few suggestions here and there, to help them use their reins properly, but for the most part, the lesson was a big success. Eventually he called a halt.

"It's time for a rest," he announced and was met with sounds of protest. "Bert will help you down. I know it's fun, but you need a break and so do the ponies. I'll give you another lesson before dinner. Right now, I thought you might like to ride to the upper pasture with me and see some Texas Longhorns."

Johnny looked perplexed. "What are those?"

"Beef cattle."

"We're not in Texas!" Sam pointed out.

"Nope, but they were brought from there to this part of the country years ago. Want to get a look at the herd?"

"Yeah!" they said with a collective voice.

He turned to the Harrises. "I'll bring them back for lunch. You can come along, or you're welcome do something else."

Ralph smiled. "If you don't mind, I think we'd like to take a walk."

"Good. Then we'll meet you back at the ranch around one o'clock."

While they talked to their children about being on their best behavior, Carson walked over to Tracy who'd once again gotten off her horse without assistance. "Are you going to ride with us?"

"Please, Mom?" Johnny's brown eyes beseeched her.

Apparently she had reservations. Maybe she hadn't been around other men since her husband's funeral and didn't feel comfortable with him or any man yet. Operating on that assumption he said, "I was going to let the kids ride in the truck bed. If you're with them, you can keep a close eye on what goes on. Those bales of hay will make a good seat for you."

She averted her eyes. "That ought to be a lot of fun."

Johnny jumped up and down with glee. "Hey, guys— we're going to ride in the back of the truck!" The other two sounded equally excited.

Pleased she'd capitulated, Carson walked over to the truck and lowered the tailgate. One by one he lifted the children inside. Before she could refuse him, he picked her up by the waist and set her down carefully. Their arms brushed against each other in the process, sending warmth through his body. After she scrambled to her feet, he closed the tailgate and hurried around to the cab.

With his pulse still racing, he started the engine and took off down the road, passing the Harrises. The children sat on the bales and clung to the sides of the truck while they called out and waved. Through the truck's rear window, Carson caught glimpses of her profile as she took in the scenery. Haunted by her utter femininity, he tried to concentrate on something else. Anything else.

There'd been a slew of women in his life from his teens on. One or two had held his interest through part of a summer, but much to his grandfather's displeasure, he'd never had the urge to settle down. It had been the same in the military.

Carson couldn't relate to the Anthony Barettas of this world, who were already happily married when deployed. Though foreign women held a certain fascination for Carson, those feelings were overshadowed by his interest in exotic places and the need to experience a different thrill.

Then came the day when his restlessness for new adventures took a literal hit from the deathly stench of war. Suffocation sucked the life out of him, extinguishing former pleasures, even his desire to be with a woman. Of no use to the military any longer, he'd been discharged early but had returned to the ranch too late to make up to his grandfather for the lost time.

Since he'd flown home from Maryland, the idea of inviting the Baretta family and others like them to the ranch had been the only thing helping him hold on to his sanity. Giving them a little pleasure might help vindicate his worthless existence, if only for a time.

Never in his wildest imagination did he expect Tony Baretta's widow to be the woman who would arouse feelings that, to his shock, must have been lying dormant since he'd become an adult.

Somehow, in his gut, he'd sensed her importance in his life from the moment they'd met at the airport. Nothing remotely like this had ever happened to him before. He couldn't explain what was going on inside him, let alone his interest in one little boy. But whatever he was experiencing was so real he could taste it and feel it.

Next Saturday they'd be flying back to Ohio. He already felt empty at the thought of it, which made no sense at all.

Chapter Four

After passing through heavily scented sage and rolling meadows, the truck wound its way up the slopes of the forest. The smell of the hay bales mingled with the fresh fragrance of the pines, filling the dry air with their distinctive perfume.

To the delight of both Tracy and the children, they spotted elk and moose along the way. Carson slowed down the truck so they could get a good look. Rabbits hopped through the undergrowth. The birdsong was so noisy among the trees, it was like a virtual aviary. Squirrels scrambled through the boughs of the pines. Chipmunks chattered. Bees zoomed back and forth.

Tracy looked all around her. The earth was alive.

Life was burgeoning on every front. She could feel it creeping into her, bringing on new sensations that were almost painful in their intensity, sensations she'd thought never to experience again.

For so long she'd felt like the flower in the little vase Johnny had brought home from school for Mother's Day. The pink rose had done its best, but after a week it had dried up. She kept it in the kitchen window as a reminder of her son's sweet gift. Every time she looked at it, she saw herself in the wasted stem and pitiful-looking petals—a woman who was all dried up and incapable of being revived.

Or so she'd thought....

After following a long curve through the trees, they came out on another slope of grassy meadow where she lost count of the cattle after reaching the two hundred mark. They came in every color. In the distance she saw a few hands and a border collie keeping an eye on the herd. Carson brought the truck to a stop and got out.

"Oh," Rachel half crooned. "Some of the mothers have babies."

Tracy had seen them. With puffy white clouds dotting the sky above the alpine pasture, it was a serene, heavenly sight of animals in harmony with nature. "They're adorable."

Carson walked around to undo the tailgate. Beneath his cowboy hat, his eyes glowed like blue topaz as he glanced at her. "Every animal, whether it be a pony or a calf, represents a miracle of nature. Don't you think?"

"Yes," she murmured, unexpectedly moved by his words and the beauty of her surroundings.

Johnny's giggle brought her head around. "Look at the funny calf. She's running away."

"Buster won't let her get far." Carson lowered the children to the ground. Tracy stayed put on her bale of hay. "Wouldn't you like to walk around with us?"

"They won't hurt you, Mom."

She chuckled. "I know. But from up here I can get some pictures of you guys first." Tracy pulled out her cell phone to make her point. "I'll join you in a minute." She didn't want Carson's help getting down. To her chagrin she still felt his touch from earlier when he'd lifted her in.

After she'd snapped half a dozen shots, she sat down on the tailgate and jumped to the ground. The children had followed Carson, who walked them through the herd, answering their myriad questions. Why were some of the calves speckled and their mothers weren't? How come they drank so much water? He was a born teacher, exhibiting more patience than she possessed.

Soon the dog ran up to them, delighting the kids. Tracy trailed behind, trying not to be too startled when some of the cows decided to move to a different spot or made long lowing sounds.

Carson cornered one of the beige-colored calves and held it so the children could pet it. Their expressions were so priceless, she pulled out her camera and took a couple of more pictures for herself and the Harrises, who would love to see these.

The hour passed quickly. When he finally announced it was time to get back to the ranch house, the children didn't want to go. He promised them they could come again in a few days.

"Do you think that calf will remember us?" Johnny wanted to know. All the children had to run to keep up with his long strides. Luckily their cowboy hats were held on with ties and didn't fall off.

As Tracy looked at Carson waiting for his answer, their gazes collided. "I wouldn't be surprised. The real question is, will you remember which calf you played with?"

"Sure," Sam piped up. "It had brown eyes."

A half smile appeared on Carson's mouth, drawing Tracy's attention when it shouldn't have. "I'm afraid they all have brown eyes. Every once in a while a blue-eyed calf is born here, but their irises turn brown after a couple of months."

Rachel stared up at him. "Do you think there might be one with blue eyes in this herd?"

"Maybe. Tell you what. The next time I bring you up here, you guys can check all the calves' eyes. I'll give you a prize if you can find a blue pair."

"Hooray!" the children cried.

On that exciting note, he lifted them into the truck and shut the tailgate without reaching for Tracy.

Perhaps he wasn't thinking when he did it, but it meant she'd be riding in the cab with him. He must have been reading her mind because he said, "Riding on top of a hay bale might work one way, but you've got more horseback riding to do and deserve a break." Flashing her a quick smile, he turned to the kids.

"That basket in the corner has water and fruit for you guys. How about handing your mom a bottle, Johnny?"

"Okay. Do you want one, too?"

"I sure do. Thanks. Your mom's going to ride in front with me. That means everyone sits down the whole time and holds on tight to the side."

"We will," they said in unison.

"That's good. We don't want any accidents."

"Please be careful," Tracy urged the kids.

"Mom—we're not babies!"

Carson's chuckle turned into a coughing spell as he helped her into the passenger side of the truck. Their fingers brushed when he handed her the bottle of water. This awareness of him was ridiculous, but all she could do was pretend otherwise.

He shut the door and went around to the driver's

side. She could still smell residual smoke from yesterday's forest fire. Carson should have been spared that.

Before he got in, he drank from his bottle. She watched the muscles working in his bronzed throat. He must have been thirsty, because he drained it. After tossing it in the basket in back, he slid behind the wheel.

She drank half of hers, not so much from thirst but because she needed to occupy herself with some activity. "What do you call the color of that calf the children were petting?"

"Slate dun."

"I knew it couldn't be beige."

In her peripheral vision, she noticed him grin. "In a herd of Longhorns you'll see about every color of the rainbow represented, including stripes and spots."

"Thank you for giving us this experience." She took a deep breath of mountain air. "There's so much to learn. Johnny's going to go home loaded with information and impress his relatives. That's saying a lot since they always sound like they know everything about everything and don't hold back expressing it."

His chuckle filled the cab. "Is he homesick yet?"

"I thought he would be. When we were flying into Jackson, I was afraid he would want to turn right around and go back. But nothing could be further from the truth. The second he caught sight of the tall dude who told him he'd take him shopping for some duds like his, he's been a changed child. For your information, tall doesn't run in the Baretta family. Neither does a Western twang."

He darted her a quick glance. "Johnny wasn't outgoing before?"

"He was…until Tony died. Since then he's been in

a reclusive state. The psychologist has been working with me to try to bring him out of his shell. When I get back to Ohio, I'm going to give him your business card and tell him to send all his trauma patients to the Teton Valley Dude Ranch. It's already doing wonders for his psyche."

"That's gratifying to hear, but let's not talk about your going home yet. You just barely got here. I'm glad we're alone so you can tell me what kinds of things he wants to do the most. I don't want him to be frightened of anything."

"Well, I can tell you right now he's crazy about Goldie and would probably spend all his days riding, pretending he's a cowboy."

"He seems to be a natural around her."

"That's because of the way you introduced him to horseback riding. You've given him back some of the confidence he's lost this last year. That was a masterful stroke when you handed him the reins and suggested he walk the pony around first so she would get used to him. In your subtle way, you sent the hint that Goldie was nervous, thereby taking the fear from Johnny.

"I held my breath waiting for him to drop the reins and run over to me. To my shock, he carried on like a trouper. When he was riding her around, he wore the biggest smile I've seen in over a year. That's your doing, Carson. You have no idea the wonders you've accomplished with him already. I'm afraid you're going to get tired of my thanking you all the time."

"That's not going to happen. If my grandpa could hear our conversation, he'd be gratified by your compliment since he was the one who taught me everything I know about horses and kids."

She bit her lip. "You miss him terribly, don't you?"

"Yes. He and my grandmother were kind, wonderful people. They didn't deserve to be burdened with a headstrong, selfish grandson so early in life."

Tracy took another drink of water. "There's that word *deserve* again. Don't you know every child is selfish? The whole world revolves around them until they grow up and hopefully learn what life's really about."

His hands tightened on the steering wheel. "Except I grew up too late. I should never have left him alone."

"Did he try to keep you from going into the Marines?"

"No. Just the opposite in fact," he said before another coughing spell ensued.

"He sounds like a wise man who knew you had to find your own path. Tony's two brothers who wanted to be police officers instead of firemen got a lot of flack from the rest of the family, especially from their father. He thought there was no other way to live, but two of his sons had other ideas. It has left resentments that seem to deepen."

"That's too bad. How did he handle Tony going into the Marines?"

"He didn't like it. But by then Tony was a firefighter and planned to come back to it when he got out of the service. As long as his sons fell in line, he was happy. To this day, he's still angry with the other two. He needed to take lessons from your grandfather."

"Unfortunately nothing removes my guilt. I was his only family left."

"It sounds like he wanted *you* to be happy. That was more important to him. He took on a sacred trust when he took over your upbringing. I feel the same way now that Tony's gone. It's up to me to guide my son. I'm terrified I'll make mistakes. What worries me is the struggle Johnny's going to have later on."

"In what way?"

"His grandfather will expect him to grow up and take his place among the Baretta firefighters. Imagine his shock when we go home and Johnny announces he's going to be a cowboy like his friend Carson when he grows up."

Her comment seemed to remove some of the stress lines around his mouth that could grow hard or soft depending on his emotions. "These are early days, Tracy. Your son's going to go through a dozen different stages before he becomes a man."

She moaned. "Let's hope he doesn't end up suffering from your problem."

His brows furrowed. "What do you mean?"

Tracy looked through the back window to make sure the children were all right.

"I've been keeping an eye on them," he murmured, reading her mind again. Of course he had. He had a handle on everything, inspiring confidence in everyone, old or young.

"I don't want Johnny to be afraid to reach out for his dreams for fear of leaving me on my own. He's especially aware of it since learning I lost my parents at eighteen. Sometimes he shows signs of being overly protective. A few months ago he told me he would never leave me and planned to take care of me all my life."

"There's a sweetness in that boy."

"Don't I know it, but I refuse to exploit it. That's one of the main reasons why I decided to accept your invitation to come to the ranch. If I don't help him to live life the way he should, then I'm failing as a mother. You and your friends have done a greater service for our family than you can possibly imagine. I know I said this before. You were inspired, and I—I'm indebted to you." Her voice caught.

He sat back in the seat. "After so much heartache, do you have any idea how much I admire you for carrying on? Tell me something. How did you continue to function after your parents were killed? I can't imagine losing them both at the same time."

"We had fantastic neighbors and friends at our church. Between them and my close friends, they became my support group and helped me while I was in college. Then I met Tony and was swept into his family."

He cast her a glance. "Swept off your feet, too?"

She nodded. "Natalie, my sister-in-law who's married to Joe, one of the out-of-favor police officers in the family, has become my closest friend. They have an eight-year-old son, Cory, who gets along famously with Johnny. I've been very blessed, so I can't complain."

After a silence Carson said, "What's the other reason you decided to accept our offer?"

"To be honest, I was becoming as much of a recluse as Johnny." She told him about the Mother's Day flower. "Your letter jerked me out of the limbo I'd been wallowing in. Once I caught sight of the Tetons in the brochure, I lost my breath. Like your stomach that flew around in the air for a week after your first flight with your grandpa, I haven't been able to get my breath back since."

"After a visit to the Tetons, some people remain in that state."

"Especially you, who came home from war struggling for yours. You and your friends have paid a heavy price. I admire you more than you know."

She'd been struggling, too, but it was from trying to keep her distance from him, which was turning out to be impossible. Tracy didn't understand everything going on inside him, but she realized that keeping her distance from him would be the wrong thing to do at the moment. Johnny was beginning to thrive. In a strange way she recognized they were all emotionally crippled because of the war and needed each other to get stronger.

"Do you mind if I ask you a personal question?"

"Go ahead."

"Why isn't there a Mrs. Lundgren?"

"You wouldn't like to hear the truth."

"Try me."

"The psychiatrist at the hospital did an evaluation on all of us. That was his first question to me. When I told him I preferred new adventures to being tied down, he told me I was an angry man."

"Angry—*you?*"

Carson laughed. "That was my response, too. He told me that was a crock. He said I'd been angry all my life because my parents died. That anger took the form of flight, whether it was sports, travel, the military. He said I was too angry to settle down. But with this illness that cramped my style, it was time I came to grips with it and let it go, or I'd self-destruct."

"And have you let it go?"

"I'm trying, but when I think of what I did to my grandfather, I can't forgive myself. There's so much I've wanted to say to him."

"Don't you think he knew why you were struggling? Did he ever try to talk to you about it?"

"Thousands of times, but I always told him we'd talk later. Of course that never happened. Then the opportunity was gone."

"As my in-laws used to tell me when I wallowed in grief over my parents' death, 'You'll be together in heaven and can talk everything over then, Tracy.' I've come to believe that. One day you'll have that talk with your grandfather."

"I'd like to believe it, but you've got more faith than I have."

Tracy sat there, pained for him and unable to do anything about it. Quiet reigned inside the cab as they drove through the sage. The children, on the other hand, were whooping it up, firing their cap guns. Johnny was becoming her exuberant child again. She had to pray it wasn't solely because of Carson.

The Harris family couldn't have come to the ranch at a better time. Tracy would involve them in as many activities as possible, because every new distraction helped.

As they drove around to the front of the ranch house, a cowboy with an impressive physique whom she hadn't seen before stood talking to some guests. He had to be the third ex-marine.

The moment he saw Carson, he left them and walked over to the truck. He removed his hat and peered in his friend's open window, allowing his green eyes to take her in. He wore his curly light-brown hair longer than the other two men and was every bit as attractive.

"Welcome to the ranch, Mrs. Baretta. We've been looking forward to your visit." His remark ended with the usual cough. The sound of it wounded Tracy because she knew at what cost they'd served their country.

"Tracy? This is Buck Summerhays. Now you've met all three amigos."

"It's a privilege, Mr. Summerhays. Johnny and I can't thank you enough for making us so welcome."

"The honor of meeting Tony Baretta's family is ours. Call me Buck."

Carson opened the door. "Come on. I want you to meet Johnny and the other two children."

While he got out, Tracy hurriedly opened her door and jumped down, not wanting any assistance. Everyone congregated at the rear of the truck. The men helped the children down, and Carson made the introductions.

Buck shut the tailgate before turning to everyone. "Where have you dudes been?"

"To see the cows," Sam spoke up.

Rachel nodded. "Next time we're going to look for calves with blue eyes. Carson's going to give us a prize if we find one."

His lips twitched. "Is that so." His gaze fell on Johnny. "Now that you've been to the pasture, what do you want to do this afternoon after lunch?"

"I'd like to ride Goldie some more."

"Who's that?"

"My pony."

"Ah." His twinkling eyes sent Carson a silent message. "I was thinking I'd take you guys on a float trip down the river."

"That sounds exciting," Tracy intervened. "How about we all do that with Buck? After dinner you can have another horseback ride before bed."

"Yeah!"

Johnny wasn't quite as enthusiastic as the other two, but he didn't put up an argument for which she was thankful. "Then come on. Let's go in and wash our hands really well. After that we'll find your parents and eat." She herded the children inside the ranch house so the men could talk in private.

CARSON NOTICED BUCK'S eyes linger on Tracy as she disappeared inside the doors. He knew what his buddy was going to say before he said it.

"You're a cool one." He switched his gaze to Carson with a secretive smile. "*Nice* has to be the understatement of all time."

"Her son's nice, too."

"I can see that." Suddenly his expression sobered. "Tony Baretta shouldn't have had to die."

His throat swelled with emotion for their suffering "Amen." After more coughing he said, "I'll park the truck around back."

"I'll come with you."

In a minute they'd washed up and entered the kitchen to eat lunch.

"How was the pack trip?"

"It went without a hitch, but I noticed there are a lot of tourists already."

"There'll be a ton more as we get into summer."

They devoured their club sandwiches. "I'm thinking that on this first float trip we'll stay away from any rapids. If they enjoy it, then we'll do a more adventurous one in a few days."

"Sounds good."

"Ross is busy fishing with another group for the afternoon. Are you going to come?" Buck eyed Carson over the rim of his coffee cup.

"No. I need to lie down for a couple of hours."

Buck frowned. "Come to think of it, you don't seem yourself. What's going on?"

Carson brought him up to speed on the forest fire. "I kept the mask on as much as possible, but I still took in too much smoke."

"You shouldn't have gone near there."

"That's what Tracy said." He could still hear the concern in her voice.

His buddy's brows lifted in surprise. "Did you tell her about the fire?"

"I had to so she wouldn't think I was abandoning Johnny. When I called her to explain, I was hacking almost as badly as when we were first brought into the hospital. If I ever needed proof of how bad it is for us, yesterday did it. None of us should ever get anywhere close to a fire if we can possibly help it."

"Tell me about it. Last night I had a few coughing spasms myself and realized I needed to stay away from the campfire."

"We need to take oxygen and inhalers with us everywhere, in case we're caught in a bad situation."

"Agreed."

"Tell Johnny and the kids I have ranch business and will meet them at the corral after dinner for another lesson. Let Willy know I'm here if an emergency arises." The part-time apprentice mechanic from Jackson alternated shifts with Susan and Patty at the front desk for the extra money.

"Will do. Take it easy." He looked worried.

Carson got up from the table. "I've learned my lesson. See you tonight."

He left the kitchen and headed for his bedroom. Though he was a little more tired than usual after yesterday's incident, he was using it as an excuse to stay away from Tracy. Carson felt like he was on a seesaw with her.

Sometimes she seemed to invite more intimate conversation, particularly when she talked about not wanting to manipulate her son's feelings. Despite the blow that had changed her life, she had a healthy desire to be the best mom possible. He felt her love for Johnny, and it humbled him.

But other times, she'd keep her distance. He didn't know how to penetrate that invisible wall she threw up, no doubt to protect herself.

She'd married into a family that kept her and Johnny close. If she'd done any dating since her husband's death, it couldn't have made much of an impact. Otherwise, she wouldn't have left Ohio to come here for a week.

He stretched out on the bed. The more he thought about it, the more he was convinced this was her first experience being around a man again in such an isolated environment. A few more days together and he'd find out if she saw him in any other light than her host while she was on vacation.

This was new territory for him, too. He needed to take it slow and easy. Like the stallion he'd broken in at nineteen, you had to become friends first. The trick was to watch and key in to all the signals before you made any kind of move. One wrong step and the opportunity could be lost for a long time. Maybe forever.

And there was Johnny.

It was one thing to be the man who taught him how to horseback ride. But it was something else again if he sensed someone was trying to get close to his mother.

She'd said Johnny showed signs of being overly protective.

No man would ever be able to replace his father. It would take her son's approval and tremendous courage on Carson's part before he could begin to establish a personal relationship with her, even if she were willing.

Last but not least would be the great obstacle of the Baretta family, who would resent another man infiltrating their ranks. Worse would be their fear of Carson influencing Tony's son. He was their beloved flesh and blood.

Frustrated, he turned on his side. His thoughts went back to a certain conversation his grandfather had initiated.

"What are you looking for in a woman?"

"That's the whole point. I'm not."

"You don't want children some day?"

"I don't know."

"One of the things I love most about you is your honesty, Carson. Wherever the military takes you, don't ever lose that quality no matter what."

"Grandpa, are you really okay about my becoming a marine?"

"The only thing I can imagine being worse than your staying home for me when you want to be elsewhere, would be for me to have to leave the ranch when it's the only place I want to be. Does that answer your question?"

Oh yes, it answered it, all right. Carson had gone to do his tour of duty until it was cut short because he could no longer perform. Then he'd come home to the birthright his grandfather had bequeathed him without asking anything in return.

What tragic irony to be back for good, wanting to tell his grandfather that, at last, he could answer those questions. He wanted that talk so badly, tears stung his eyes. But it was too late to tell him what this woman and her son already meant to him.

When he couldn't stand it any longer, he got up to shower and change clothes. There was always ranch business that required his attention. Work had proved to be the panacea to keep most of his demons at bay. But when he left his room, instead of heading for the den, he turned in the other direction and kept on walking right out the back door to his truck.

After reaching the barn, he saddled Blueberry. On his way out he saw Bert and told him he'd be back at seven to give the children another riding lesson. The other man said he'd have the ponies ready.

Carson thanked him and rode off. His horse needed the exercise, and needing the release, Carson rode hard to a rise overlooking the Snake River. In his opinion, this spot on the property captured the view of the grand-daddy Teton at its most magnificent angle. He'd often wondered why his ancestor, Silas Lundgren, hadn't chosen to build the original ranch house here.

While he sat astride Blueberry, his mind's eye could imagine a house of glass, bringing the elements inside every room. Not a large house. Just the right size for a family to grow. Maybe a loft a little boy and his dog would love. From their perch they could watch a storm settle in over the Tetons, or follow the dive of an eagle intent on its prey.

The master bedroom would have the same view, with the added splendor of a grassy meadow filled with wild-flowers coming right up to the windows. While she marveled over the sight, he would marvel over *her*, morning, noon and night.

A cough eventually forced him to let go of his vision. When he checked his watch, he saw it was almost seven o'clock. He had to give his horse another workout in order not to be too late.

As he came galloping up to the corral, he saw Tracy's hair gleaming in the evening rays of the sun. She was surrounded by both families, mounted and ready for another lesson. He brought Blueberry to a sliding stop.

"Wow—" Johnny exclaimed from the top of Goldie. "Will you teach me how to do that? It was awesome!"

Chapter Five

The man and horse truly were one.

Talk about rugged elegance personified in its purest form!

Except for Johnny, everyone else sitting on their mounts was speechless. Tracy realized she was staring and looked away, but she'd never get that picture of him out of her mind. The quintessential cowboy had been indelibly inscribed there.

"If you'll follow me," came his deep voice, "we'll take a short ride past the cabins. On the way back, I have a surprise for you."

"Won't you tell us?" Sam called to him.

"No," his sister chided him. "Then it won't be a surprise."

Tracy exchanged an amused glance with the Harrises. The three of them rode behind the children. Johnny caught up to Carson. Two cowboys—one short, one tall—both wearing black Stetsons. She would love to hear their conversation, but the only sound drifting back was the occasional cough.

To see her son riding so proudly on his pony next to his mentor brought tears to her eyes. They'd been here such a short time, yet already he was loving this and showed no fear. Coming to the Tetons had been the right thing to do!

In the last twelve hours she hadn't heard him talk once about his father. In truth, Tony hadn't been actively in her thoughts, either. Neither she nor Johnny had memories here. The new setting and experiences had pushed the past to the background for a little while. As Natalie had reminded her, this was what the right kind of vacation was supposed to do for you.

Tracy hadn't believed it was possible, but this evening she was confronted with living proof that Johnny was enjoying life again. So was she. The old adage about a mother being as happy as her saddest child could have been coined with her and her son in mind. But not tonight. *Not tonight.*

At one point, Carson turned his horse around. Flashing everyone a glance he said, "We're going to head back now. The first person to figure out my surprise gets to choose the video for us to watch in the game room afterward."

The children cried out with excitement and urged their horses around, which took a little doing. Carson gave them some pointers. Tracy listened to his instructions so she wouldn't be the only one who had trouble handling her horse.

Pretty soon they were all facing west. Sam's hand went up like he was in school. Johnny's hand followed too late.

"Tell us what you think, Sam."

"The mountains have turned into giants!"

"That's what *I* was going to say," Johnny muttered. Tracy hoped he wouldn't pout.

Carson's horse danced in place. "They do look pretty imposing, but I'm still waiting for the special answer."

"*I* know."

"Go ahead, Rachel."

"The sun has gone down behind them, lighting up the whole sky with colors."

"Congratulations! It's the greatest sight this side of the Continental Divide." Carson lifted his hat in a sweeping gesture, delighting her. "The lovely young cowgirl on Mitzi wins the prize."

After the grownups clapped, Monica let out a sigh. "It's probably the most beautiful sunset I've ever seen, and we've watched thousands of them over the ocean in Florida, haven't we, Ralph."

"You can say that again."

Tracy agreed with them, especially the way the orangey-pink tones painted Carson's face before his hat went back on.

A sly smile broke the corner of his mouth. "First person to reach the corral wins a new currycomb."

Sam's brows wrinkled. "A curry what?"

"A kind of comb to clean your ponies after a ride. They love it."

"Come on!" Johnny shouted and made some clicking sounds with his tongue the way Carson had shown him. Goldie obeyed and started walking. In her heart of hearts, Tracy wanted her son to win.

In the end, the ponies hurried after Goldie. They kept up with each other and rode in together. Carson smiled at them. "You *all* win."

"Yay!"

While Bert helped the children down and unsaddled their ponies, Carson went into the barn and brought them each their prizes. Once he'd dismounted, he removed the tack from his horse and showed them how to move the round metal combs in circles. They got to work with a diligence any parents could be proud of. Then they watered the horses and gave them oats.

He was a master teacher. Tonight they'd learned lessons they'd never forget—how to appreciate a beautiful sunset, how to care for an animal, how to handle competition. The list went on and on, increasing her admiration for him.

"Who wants a ride back to the house?"

"We do!"

"Then come on." He punctuated it with a cough. "There's room for everyone in the back."

The men lifted the children. While Ralph helped Monica, Carson picked up Tracy. This time the contact of their thighs brushing against each other flowed through her like a current of electricity. She tried to suppress her gasp but feared he'd heard it.

On the short trip through the sage, the kids sang. They sounded happy, and Tracy started singing with them. It took her back to her youth. She'd had a pretty idyllic childhood. When Carson pulled the truck up in front of the house, she didn't want the moment to end.

Ralph moved first and helped everyone down, including Tracy. That was good. She didn't dare get that close to Carson again tonight. He'd kept the engine idling and said he'd see them in a minute before he took off around the back of the house. Everyone hurried inside to wash up.

Soon Carson joined them, bringing sodas from the kitchen. He sat on one of the leather chairs while the rest of them gathered round the big screen on two large leather couches. Fortunately, they had the game room to themselves.

To the boys' disappointment, Rachel chose *The Princess Bride,* but Tracy enjoyed it and got the feeling all the grownups did, too. Before it was over, both Sam and Johnny's eyes had closed. Ralph took his son home, leaving Rachel to finish the film with her mom.

Carson eyed Tracy. "Johnny's had a big day, too. I'll walk you to your cabin."

Her heart jumped at the idea of being alone with him, but to turn him down would cause attention. Instead, she said good-night to the others and followed him out of the ranch house while he held Johnny's hand. Her son was pretty groggy all the way to the cabin.

Tracy had to laugh when he staggered into the bedroom. Carson looked on with a smile as she got him changed into pajamas and tucked him into bed without a visit to the bathroom. "My son is zonked."

He nodded. "Johnny's gone nonstop all day. This altitude wears a man out."

She turned off the light and they went into the front room where another bout of coughing ensued. Tracy darted him an anxious glance. "You should be in bed, too."

Carson cocked his head. "Is that your polite way of trying to get me to leave?"

She hadn't expected that question. "No—" she answered rather too emotionally, revealing her guilt. "Not at all."

"Good, because I rested earlier and now I'm not tired." He removed his hat and tossed it on the table.

"Please help yourself to any of the snacks." She

folded her legs under her and sank down on the end of the couch.

"Don't mind if I do." He reached for the pine nuts. The next thing she knew, he'd lounged back in one of the overstuffed chairs, extending his long legs. "We need to have a little talk."

Alarmed, she sat forward. "Is there something wrong?"

"I don't know. You tell me." Between narrowed lids his eyes burned a hot blue, searing her insides.

"I don't understand."

He stopped munching. "I think you do. You need to be honest with me. Are you uncomfortable around me?"

She swallowed with difficulty, looking everywhere except at him. "If I've made you feel that way, then it's purely unintentional. I'm so sorry."

"So you do admit there's a problem."

Tracy got to her feet. "Not with you," she murmured.

"Johnny, then?"

Her eyes widened. "How can you even ask me that?"

The question seemed to please him because the muscles in his face relaxed. "Does your family wish you hadn't come?"

"I know my in-laws were astounded you and your friends had made such an opportunity available in honor of their son. They were really touched, but I believe they thought Johnny would want to turn right around and come home."

One brow dipped. "Is that what you thought, too?"

"When I first told Johnny about the letter, he said he didn't want to go. I knew why. Wyoming sounded too far away."

"What did you do to change his mind?"

"I asked him if he at least wanted to see the brochure you sent. He agreed to take a look. The second he saw that photo of the Tetons, he was blown away."

Their gazes fused. "Those mountains have a profound effect on everyone."

"Then he wanted to know about white water. But something extraordinary happened when he saw that gigantic elk with the huge *horns*..." Carson chuckled. "He looked at me and I felt his soul peer into mine before he asked me if I wanted to go. He always asks me first how I feel when he wants something but is afraid to tell me.

"I still wasn't sure how he'd feel after he got here. In retrospect, even if he'd wanted to turn right around, that airplane trip from Salt Lake would have put him off flying for a while."

Carson's smile widened, giving her heart another workout.

"My sister-in-law Natalie thought it was a fantastic opportunity and urged me to accept the invitation, but I don't know how my in-laws really felt about my taking their grandson to another part of the continent."

The tension grew. "Now that you've ruled out all of that, we're back to my original question, the one you still haven't answered."

Naturally he hadn't forgotten where this conversation had been headed and wouldn't leave the cabin while he waited for the truth. "As you've probably divined, *I'm* the problem."

"Why?"

He had a side to him that could be blunt and direct when the occasion demanded. It caught her off guard. "I guess there was one thing I hadn't thought about before we left. After we arrived here, it took me by surprise."

"Explain what you mean." He wasn't going to let this go.

She took a fortifying breath. "I assumed we'd be coming to a vacation spot with all the activities mentioned, but it has turned out to be…more."

"In what regard?"

"I—I didn't expect the one-on-one treatment," her voice faltered.

"From me and my buddies?"

"Yes."

He got to his feet. "But that was the whole point."

Tracy nodded. "I realize that now. But for some reason, I didn't think your business enterprise meant it would be a hands-on experience involving you so personally."

His brows met in a frown. "A dude ranch is meant to cater to the individual. If the three of us weren't here, there'd be others giving you the same attention. After losing your husband, does it bother you to be around other males again? Is that what this is about? I've half suspected as much."

She felt her face growing red as an apple.

"Have you even been out with a man since he died?"

"I've been to faculty functions with men, but they've always been in groups."

"In other words, no, you haven't."

"No," she whispered.

"And now you're suddenly thrown together with three bachelors practically 24/7." He put his hands on his hips in a totally male stance. "I get it. And I'll tell you something."

At this juncture, she felt like too much of a fool to know what to say, so she let him talk.

"I haven't been out with a woman since I was transported from the Middle East to Walter Reed Medical Center. When we were discharged, I felt like I was going home to die. The only thing that kept me going was this plan I dreamed up with Ross and Buck to bring a little happiness to the families who were suffering the loss of a husband and father.

"Lady—when I saw you walk through the airport terminal, I was as unprepared as you were. It was one thing to visualize Anthony Baretta's widow and his son in my mind, but quite another to be confronted with the sight of you in the flesh."

Tracy lowered her head. "After thinking of you in the abstract, the sight of you was pretty overwhelming, too," she confessed. "I guess we'd been picturing three marines in uniform whom we'd get to meet at some point during our stay so we could thank you. Instead, we were greeted by the king of the cowboys, as Johnny refers to you in private. He wasn't prepared, either, and clung to me for a long moment."

"I remember," he said in a husky-sounding voice before another cough came on. "From a distance, he was your husband's replica. That is, until I saw both your faces close up."

She eyed him covertly. Close up or at a distance, Carson Lundgren was no man's replica. He was an original with a stature to match the mountains outside the cabin door. "I'm glad we had this conversation. I feel much better about everything."

"So do I. From now on we each understand where the other is coming from. It'll make everything easier."

Not necessarily. Not while her pulse was racing too hard.

"Pardon the expression, but you and Johnny are our guinea pigs in this venture. The next family we've invited will be arriving next month. Because of you, we'll be much better prepared for the emotional upheaval created by war, whatever it is. Thank you for being honest with me. It means more than you know."

"Thank you for a wonderful day."

His eyes deepened in color. "There's more to come tomorrow, if you're up for it. But after Johnny's experience flying into Jackson, maybe not."

She took an extra breath. "You're talking about a hot-air-balloon ride? The kind mentioned in your brochure?"

"It's an unprecedented way to experience the Teton Valley. Buck will be taking some groups up."

"I'd love to go, but I'll have to feel out Johnny in the morning before breakfast. If it's mentioned at the table and the other children want to g—"

"I hear you," he broke in. "Johnny might be afraid, but will be too scared to admit it. I don't want to put him under any pressure. When you know how he feels, call the front desk. They'll put you through to me. If necessary, I'll give Buck a heads-up."

"Thank you. You have unusual understanding of children."

"I was a child once and had my share of fears to deal with. Peer pressure was a killer. I'm thinking that if he doesn't like the balloon idea, then we'll take a longer horseback ride tomorrow and enjoy an overnight campout on the property." He put his hat back on, ready to leave. For once she wasn't ready to let him go, but she had to.

"I can tell you right now he'll be in ecstasy over that option."

"Good. If it turns out to be successful, then he'll probably be ready to do another one in Teton Park. We'll take the horses up to String Lake. It's a great place to swim and hike around."

"Sounds heavenly."

She had to remember that he was working out the rest of their vacation agenda rather than making a date with her. Yet that's what it felt like. Her reaction was ridiculous considering she was a mother of twenty-seven instead of some vulnerable nineteen-year-old.

The only time she'd ever felt like this before was when she'd driven to Cleveland with some of her girlfriends from college. They were having a picnic at Lakefront State Park when a crew of firefighters had pulled up to eat their lunch and toss a football around. The cutest guy in the group started flirting with her. Mr. Personality. He could talk his way in or out of anything. Tony was a mover who told her after one date that he was going to marry her.

When she thought of Carson, there was no point of comparison because he wasn't pursuing her. That was why she was a fool trying to make one.

"All we've talked about is Johnny's pleasure. Since this vacation is for you, too, why don't you tell me something you'd like to do while you're here?"

She laughed gently. "If he's happy, then that's what makes me happy, but I have to admit I enjoy riding. I had no idea I'd like it this much. You're a great teacher."

"That's nice to hear."

"It's true." After a brief pause because she suddenly felt tongue-tied, she wished him goodnight. He tipped his hat and left.

Tracy closed the door behind him and locked it. Though he'd walked away as if he was glad the air had been cleared, she was afraid she'd offended him. It was humiliating to realize he'd figured out her lame hang-up about being around a man again before she'd articulated it.

To make certain she didn't get the wrong idea about him, Carson had revealed his own surprise at meeting *her*. Then, in the nicest way possible, he'd let her have it by spelling it out she wasn't the only one suffering emotional fallout from the war.

When she finally got into bed, she felt worse than a fool.

WHEN TRACY STEPPED out of the shower, she could hear Johnny talking to someone. Throwing on a robe, she walked into the bedroom just as he put her cell phone on the bedside table.

"Who was that, honey?"

"Grandma and Grandpa."

"Why didn't you tell me?"

"Because you were in the bathroom. They said they'd call back tomorrow morning 'cos they were in a hurry."

"How are they?"

"Fine. They want to see me ride Goldie. I told them Carson's been teaching me and took us to get my cowboy outfit and cap gun." He ran over and gave her an exuberant hug. "I'm having the best time of my whole life!"

"I'm so glad."

"When are we going home?"

Uh-oh. "Next Saturday morning. Why? Are you missing them too much?"

"No. What's today?"

"Monday." Time was flying.

She could hear him counting in his head. "So we have five more days?"

"Yes."

"Goody! I don't want to go home. I can't leave Goldie."

Tracy knew he'd said it in the heat of the moment, and she was happy about it, but the implication for what it might portend for the future stole some of her happiness.

Though home would be wonderfully familiar to her son after they got back, he would suffer his first attack of culture shock, because nothing in Sandusky or Cleveland compared remotely to Wyoming's Teton Valley.

"Mom? Do you like it here?"

That was one of his trick questions. He needed to find out what *she* really thought before he expressed exactly what *he* thought. No doubt her in-laws had asked him the same question.

She ruffled his hair. "What do you think? I got on a horse, didn't I?"

"Yes," he answered in a quiet tone.

Something else was definitely on his mind, but she didn't know if he was ready to broach it yet, so she asked him a question. "How would you like to go up in a hot-air balloon today and see the whole area?"

Tracy had to wait a long time for the answer she knew was coming. "Do you?" That lackluster question told her everything.

"I don't know. There are so many things to do here, it's hard to pick. We could fish or swim, or go on a hike."

No response.

"Maybe we ought to have a break and drive into town to do some sightseeing. I'll buy you some more caps."

"I don't want to do that," he muttered.

"Or…we could go horseback riding. I like it."

He shot up in her bed. His dark brown eyes had ignited. "I *love* it."

His reaction was no surprise, but the intensity of it had come from some part deep inside of him. "Then it's settled. Hurry and have your bath. After we're dressed we'll have breakfast and walk over to the corral."

Johnny pressed a big kiss right on her mouth. That told her everything she needed to know before he scrambled out of her bed to the bathroom. When he was out of earshot, she called the front desk and was quickly put through to Carson.

"Good morning, Tracy." His voice sounded an octave lower, sending vibrations through her. Maybe it was due to his coughing, or maybe he sounded like that when he first awakened. "What's the verdict for today?"

She smiled. "Surely you don't need to ask."

"Well that answer suits me just fine, since there's nothing I'd rather do than be on the back of a horse. I'll tell Buck to go on without you. After you've eaten breakfast, I'll come by the cabin. You'll need saddlebags to pack your things to stay overnight and go swimming."

"Swimming?"

"Yes. We'll be camping next to a small lake on the property. If Johnny has a camera, tell him to bring it.

He'll have a field day taking pictures of the wildlife I was talking to you about."

An unbidden thrill of excitement ran through her. "We'll hurry."

FORTY-FIVE MINUTES later Carson swung by the cabin in the Jeep, having sent some of the hands to the lake to make preparations for everyone. Johnny was outside shooting off caps.

"Carson!" Like a heat-seeking missile, Tracy's boy came running in his cowboy hat. "Mom said we're going on a campout!" He clasped him around the waist, hugging him with such surprising strength, his hat fell off. Johnny had never been this demonstrative before.

Without hesitation, Carson hugged him back. "We sure are, partner," he answered in an unsteady voice, loving the feel of those young arms clinging to him. Nothing had ever felt so good.

As he started coughing, he looked up and saw Tracy on the porch step, but was unable to read her expression. She'd told him Johnny was protective of her. Without saying more than that, Carson got the point. Her son had a tendency to guard her.

But she couldn't have missed witnessing his exuberance with Carson just now. It had probably shocked her as much as it had him. Needing to return the situation to normal as fast as possible, he reached in the back of the Jeep and handed Johnny some gear.

"These saddlebags are for your stuff. The bigger one is for your mom. Will you take them into the cabin so she can pack what you need?"

"Sure."

"Remember to bring a jacket."

He flashed him a huge smile. "I will. I'll be right back."

Carson kept his distance and lounged against the side of the Jeep to wait. Pretty soon they came out. Johnny carried both bags and handed them to Carson to put in the back. It warmed his heart to see the boy was a quick learner.

"Can I ride in front, Mom?"

"If it's all right with Carson."

"Anything goes around here. Come on." He opened both passenger doors for them, avoiding eye contact with her. So much for the talk they'd had last night. Considering he was more aware of her than ever, it had accomplished absolutely nothing. "We'll drive to the barn and mount up."

"How come Rachel and Sam didn't come to breakfast?"

In the rearview mirror he noticed a pair of hazel eyes fastened on him.

"They ate early and went on an activity with Buck. He'll bring them to the camp later, but they won't be riding up with us."

"Hooray!"

"Johnny—" his mother scolded. "That wasn't nice to say."

"I'm sorry, but their ponies always come right up to mine."

Carson glanced at him in surprise. "So you noticed." He had natural horse sense. Everything the boy said and did pleased him.

"Yeah. They get in the way."

"I know what you mean. When it happens again, I'll teach you a simple trick so they'll leave Goldie alone."

"Thanks! How come they do that?"

"Have you ever heard of the three blind mice who hung around together?"

Johnny giggled. "Yes."

"That's what the ponies do, because they're friends. When you're on Goldie, you have to show them who's the boss."

"But how?"

"Have you ever heard the expression giddyup?"

"Yup."

"Well, you're going to practice saying that to Goldie today. And when you say it, you're going to nudge her sides with your heels. That'll make her go faster. Pretty soon she'll start to go faster every time you say the word and you won't need to use your heels. When she understands, then you wait until you're riding with the other kids. If their ponies start to crowd in on you, just call out 'giddyup' and see what happens."

"But what if that makes the other ponies go faster, too?"

Carson threw his head back and laughed, producing another cough. When it subsided, he could still hear Tracy's laughter. "That's a very astute question, partner. In all probability it will, so you'll have to ride even harder and make a lot of noise. But you'll also need to be prepared to pull on the reins so you don't lose control."

"That's going to be fun!"

Johnny bounced up and down on the seat all the way to the barn where their horses and pony were saddled. Carson parked the Jeep outside before grabbing the bags, including his own. He fastened a set behind each saddle while Bert helped Tracy and Johnny to mount.

Bert waved them off. "Have a good ride!"

"Thanks. We will!" Johnny called back. "See ya tomorrow, Bert."

"Okay, young fella."

Add another fan to Johnny Baretta's list. To charm old Bert wasn't an easy feat. So far the waitresses and desk staff, not to mention Carson's buddies, found him delightful.

Carson hadn't personally known Anthony Baretta, but he had a reputation in their division for being well liked and easy to get along with. Like father, like son.

Carson led them along a track through the sage in a northeastly direction. Johnny followed, and Tracy brought up the rear. When they'd been going for a while, he fell back alongside Johnny and told him to start working on Goldie.

The first few times the boy said giddyup, he didn't use his heels fast enough and nothing happened. Johnny's frustration started to build.

"You have to be patient and listen to Carson, honey."

"But I *am* listening, Mom."

"Sure you are," Carson encouraged him. "The trick is to use your heels at exactly the same time you call out. Try a louder voice the next time."

"What if it doesn't work?"

"Then you keep trying until it does. Did I ever tell you about the first time I learned to ride a bull?"

"No. What happened?"

"I was training for the junior bull-riding competition. It was awful. I got unseated so fast every time, I was ready to cry."

"Did you?" came the solemn question.

"Almost. But then I looked at my grandpa. He was

just standing there by the gate with a smile, telling me to try it again."

"What did you do?"

"I got so mad, I walked back behind the barrier and climbed on another bull. When the gate opened, I concentrated on what I'd learned, and guess what? I stayed on long enough for the other cowboys watching to clap."

"I bet your grandpa was happy."

"Yup, but not as happy as I was."

"I think I'll wait a little while before I try again," he announced.

Carson understood Johnny's sentiments well enough. He'd been there and done that many times before. "That's fine. We're in no hurry."

Tracy drew up along the other side of her son. "I hope you don't wait too long. We're coming to the forest."

Carson could sense her desire for Johnny to conquer this moment. It managed to fire her son who got a determined look on his cute face. All of a sudden they heard a loud giddyup rend the air and Goldie took off trotting. Johnny let out a yelp.

"Pull on the reins and she'll stop."

To Carson's delight, Johnny had the presence of mind to follow through and ended up doing everything right. He turned his pony toward them. "She *minded* me."

"Yup." Carson couldn't be more proud if Johnny were his own son. "Now she knows who's boss."

"You were amazing, honey!"

"Thanks."

When Tracy beamed like that, her beauty took Carson's breath. She stared at him through glistening eyes. "You've worked magic with him."

"He's *your* son, don't forget."

"I can't take any credit for this. His confidence level is through the roof. How do I thank you?"

"With that smile, you already have."

"Hey, you guys—aren't you coming?"

Johnny's question broke the odd stillness that had suddenly enveloped them. Both their shoulders shook with laughter at the same time. "What's the hurry?" Carson called out when he could find his voice.

"I want to keep riding."

"You mean you're not tired yet?"

"Tired? No way! Come on! Goldie wants to keep going."

"We're coming. Since you're in the lead, we'll continue to follow you."

"What if I get lost?"

"Hey, partner—we can't get lost. This is my back yard."

"Back yard!" Johnny laughed hysterically. "You're so funny, Carson."

He blinked. "No one in the world has ever said that to me before."

"Sometimes you really are," Tracy concurred. "As my son has found out, it's a very appealing side of you."

Carson felt an adrenalin rush. *Is that what you think too, Tracy?*

"Mom? How come you guys keep talking?"

He heard her clear her throat. "Because we're waiting for you to get going." She darted Carson an amused glance.

"Oh."

With less trouble than he'd demonstrated earlier, Johnny turned the palomino around and headed into the forest. The three of them were on the move once more, this time with Tracy at Carson's side. But after they got into the thick of the pines, the trail became less discernible in spots. Carson pulled alongside Johnny. His mother stayed right behind them.

"Seen any bad guys yet?"

"No, but I'm keeping a lookout."

"Got your mustang handy?"

"It's in my pocket. How far is the lake?"

"We wind up the slope for two more miles."

"What's it called?"

"I call it Secret Lake."

"Who else knows about it?"

"Only my best friends."

"You mean Ross and Buck?"

"That's right. And a few others. It's my favorite place. I can't let just anybody come up here. Otherwise it wouldn't be a secret."

Johnny looked over at him with those serious dark eyes. "Thanks for bringing me. I'm having the funnest time of my whole life."

Chapter Six

It was the second time Tracy's son had expressed the very sentiment she felt. She had to admit she was enjoying this trip a lot more than she'd anticipated. But along with this newfound excitement, her guilt was increasing.

Strictly speaking, it wasn't the guilt some war widows experienced, making them cling to the memory of their husbands. The love she and Tony shared would always be in her heart. They'd talked about the possibility of his dying, and she'd promised him she would move on if—heaven forbid—something happened to him. Since that horrible day, she'd been doing her best to make a full life for herself and Johnny.

This was a different kind of guilt, because she *didn't* feel guilty about enjoying Carson's company. To be honest, she was attracted to him. Very attracted.

Her biggest fear was that he'd already sensed it. Last night he'd sounded relieved after they'd had their talk. As he'd explained, when he and his friends had put their plan into action, they'd done it purely to brighten up the lives of a few families affected by the war.

Neither Carson nor his friends wanted or expected some love-starved woman with a child to come on to them because she'd lost her husband. The thought had to have crossed his mind when they'd first met at the airport.

According to Carson, the three men had been bachelors when they'd joined the Marines. And they were still living that lifestyle outside of this special project that was bringing so much joy to Johnny's life. Since Tracy couldn't help what they were thinking, there was no point in being embarrassed. What she needed to do was be friends with all of them, the way she was with Tony's brothers. That was going to be especially hard when she was around Carson, but she could do it. And she would!

"Mom—there's the lake!"

Johnny's exultant cry jolted her back to the moment. They'd moved on ahead of her. "Good for you for finding it! Does it look like Lake Erie with lots of barges and a lighthouse?" she teased.

"Heck, no. It's little, with pine trees all around it."

She smiled. "Can you see any fish?"

"Can you?" she heard him ask Carson. *Oh, Johnny.* Her son was so predictable.

"See all those dark things moving around?"

"Yeah."

"The lake is full of rainbow trout."

"I don't see their rainbows."

"You will when you catch one." Carson was ever the patient teacher. "We'll cook it for your dinner tonight."

"Won't there be anything else to eat?" was her son's forlorn reply.

Carson's laughter warmed new places inside her. "We've got lots of stuff."

"That's good."

Tracy drew closer to them.

"Hey—I can see some tents and a table! Someone else is camping here." He didn't sound happy about that.

Carson laughed again. "Yup. That someone is *you*, partner. Those tents have already been set up for us."

"Whoa!"

"Maybe you'd like to sleep in that three-man tent with Sam and Rachel."

"Oh, yeah. I forgot they were coming. Where will you sleep?"

"Right next to you guys in my tent."

"What about my mom?"

"There's a tent for her and one for the Harrises. The one on the end is for Buck."

"But there are six tents."

"Yup. The extra one is where we keep the food and all the supplies we'll need. After we take care of the horses, we'll fix ourselves some lunch."

"Goody."

Their entertaining conversation was music to Tracy's ears. She finally broke through the heavy cover of pines to discover a small body of deep green water bathed by the sun. "This place looks enchanted."

While Carson put out some hay and water for the horses, he slanted her a hooded look. "It is."

She felt a shiver run through her. They'd already dismounted and he'd removed the saddles and bags.

"Come over here, Mom. I'll tie your reins to this tree the way Carson showed me."

"Such wonderful service deserves a kiss." She got down off her horse and planted one on her son's cheek.

"The latrine is around the other side in the trees, away from the camping area," he informed her.

Latrine. Since their arrival in Jackson, Johnny's vocabulary must have increased by a couple of hundred words at least. He was becoming a veritable fount of knowledge.

"Thanks. I'll keep that in mind." Without being asked, Tracy picked up their bags. "I'll take these."

"Put mine in the big tent."

"Didn't you forget to say something?"

"Oh, yeah. Please. I forgot."

"I know, but it's so much nicer when you remember."

Carson's eyes smiled at her before she started walking along the tree-lined shore toward the tents pitched some distance away. She undid the tie on the screen and entered the big one where three sleeping bags and extra blankets were rolled out. It was getting hot out, but the temperature inside was still pleasant.

She emptied his saddlebag and put his things in little stacks against the side of his sleeping bag. Then she left and picked out one of the other tents for herself. It didn't take her long to unpack.

When she emerged, she discovered Carson putting out picnic food on the camp table beneath some pine boughs to give them shade. Johnny had the duty of setting up the camp chairs.

Tracy approached them and looked all around. "With the smell of the pines so strong, this is what I call heaven on earth." She eyed her son. "Do you know how lucky we are, Johnny? Can you believe Carson and his friends have gone to all this trouble for us? We're going to have to think of something really special to do for them."

"I know."

They settled down to eat.

"Guess what?" Carson said after swallowing his second roast beef sandwich. "You've already done something special."

Johnny stopped chewing on his sandwich. "No, we haven't."

"Want to bet? You accepted our invitation to come. We hoped you and your mom would like the idea." He darted her a penetrating glance. "That's all the payment we needed."

Carson.

"At first I didn't want to." Her son was nothing if not honest.

"I don't blame you. I'd have been scared to go someplace where I'd never been before. I think you were very brave to come."

"I'm not brave, but my mom is."

"She sure is." In an unexpected gesture, Carson pulled out his phone and clicked on the photo gallery. "Now take a look at this." He handed it to Johnny.

"That's me riding Goldie!"

"Yup. How many kids do you know your age who can go on a trail ride in the mountains on their own pony?" Tracy hadn't seen him take a picture. She was amazed. Had he taken one of her, too?

Johnny's brown gaze switched from the photo to study Carson. "I don't know any."

"Neither do I. So don't ever tell me Tony Baretta's son isn't brave." Carson's expression grew serious. "You're just like your dad and I'm proud to know you."

The conviction in his tone shook Tracy to the core and affected Johnny to the point of tears. They didn't fall, but they shimmered on the tips of his lashes with every heartbeat. "I'm proud of you, too. You're sick all the time and still do *everything*."

If Tracy wasn't mistaken, Carson's eyes had a suspicious sheen. As for herself, a huge lump had lodged in her throat.

"If everyone's finished eating, what do you say we put the rest of the food in the bear locker and go for a swim? Remember we have to fasten it tight. Occasionally a black bear or a grizzly forages through this area, but unlikely you'll ever see one."

Johnny looked at Tracy. "Don't worry, Mom. Carson brought bear spray. He'll keep us safe."

She lifted her gaze to a pair of blue eyes that blinded her with their intensity. "I have no doubt of it."

The three of them made short work of cleaning up and went to their respective tents to change into their bathing suits. When Johnny was dressed, he came running with his beach sandals and towel to her tent. She'd put a beach cover-up over her one-piece blue floral suit.

Before leaving Sandusky, she'd searched half a dozen shops to find something modest. Other women didn't mind being scantily clad, but she wasn't comfortable walking around like that.

Once she'd covered them in sunscreen, she grabbed her towel and they both left the tent in search of Carson. He'd beaten them to the shore and was blowing up a huge inner tube with a pump. Johnny squealed in delight.

The only thing more eye-catching than the sight of this pristine mountain lake was Carson Lundgren dressed in nothing more than his swimming trunks. Tracy had trouble not staring at such an amazing, hard-packed specimen of male beauty.

She felt his keen gaze play over her before he said, "Johnny? I want you to wear the life jacket I left on the table. Even if you're a good swimmer, I'll feel much better if you wear it while we're out here. Don't be fooled by this lake. You can only wade in a few feet, then it drops off fast to thirty feet."

Johnny's dark head swung around. "Okay." He ran over and put it on. Tracy made sure he'd fastened it correctly.

"I think we're ready!" Carson announced. He tossed the tube in the water, then dove in and came up in the center with a lopsided smile that knocked her off balance. "Come on in, and we'll go for a ride."

Johnny needed no urging and started running. Tracy threw off her cover-up and followed him in. "Oh—this water's colder than I thought!"

"It's good for you," Carson said, and then promptly coughed. The moment was so funny she was still laughing when he helped her and Johnny to grab on to the tube. Once they were all comfortable, he propelled them around.

They must have been out there close to an hour, soaking up the sun and identifying wildlife. Sometimes they swam away from the tube. Carson flew through the water like a fish and played games with them. When everyone was exhausted, they went back to shore to dry off and get a cold drink.

"I think it's time for a little rest."

"But Mom, I have to go talk to Goldie. She's missed me."

"You can see her in a little while. Come on. It's time to get out of the sun."

"What are you going to do, Carson?"

He'd been coughing. "I've got a few phone calls to make, partner. It won't be long before Buck arrives with the Harrises."

Tracy didn't know how he was able to spend so much time with them when he had the whole operation of his cattle ranch to worry about. "Thank you for another wonderful day, Carson."

He flicked her a shuttered glance. "It's only half over."

She knew that, yet the fact that he'd mentioned it filled her with fresh excitement. With an arm around Johnny, Tracy walked him to her tent, but stopped by his to get him a change of clothes. Once he was dressed, he lay down on top of her roomy sleeping bag. After she got dressed, she joined him. In two seconds, he was asleep.

Tracy lay there wondering if Carson's calls were all business. Since he'd come home from war, surely he'd been with women he'd met in Jackson or through his business contacts, even if it hadn't been an official date. That would go for his friends, too. Any woman lucky enough to capture his interest would be wondering why he hadn't been as available lately.

When she realized where her thoughts had wandered, she sat up, impatient with herself for caring what he did in his off time. She was supposed to be thinking of him as a friend, but her feelings weren't remotely like anything she felt for her brothers-in-law.

He would have been a charmer during the years he was competing in the rodeo. He had to be driving a lot of women crazy, these days, too. Carson was driving one woman crazy right here on the ranch and she didn't know what to do about it. Tracy had to admit those blue eyes and the half smile he sometimes flashed were playing havoc with her emotions.

After she'd met Tony, nothing had kept her from responding to him in an open, free way. Now, she had a son who came first in her life and the situation with Carson was so different it was almost painful. If he had feelings for her—sometimes, when he looked at her, she felt that he did—he hadn't acted on them. But then again, he was naturally kind and generous. She didn't dare read more into a smile or an intense look than was meant. He'd told her that she and Johnny were their guinea pigs.

The daunting thought occurred to her that Carson's emotions weren't invested, which explained why he never did anything overtly personal. Next month, another family devastated by the war would be arriving. He and his friends would welcome them and be as kind and attentive as they'd been to Johnny and her.

Maybe he'd meet a widow this summer who would be so desirable to him, he'd reach out to her because he couldn't help himself. Tracy groaned. What kind of woman might she be?

Tomorrow was Tuesday, and they only had four more days here. With her attraction to Carson growing, she'd found herself dreading the march of time, just like Johnny. But it suddenly dawned on her that without some signal from him, those days would seem like a lifetime.

Another worse thought intruded when she heard voices in the distance. Johnny heard them, too, and sat up, rubbing his eyes. She reached for her watch, which she'd taken off to go swimming. It was four-thirty. Buck appeared to have arrived with the others.

What if Carson had picked up on certain vibes from Tracy and had been including the Harris family in all their activities to keep everything on an even keel?

Was it true?

Maybe she was wrong, since she didn't know Carson's mind, but she cringed to think it could be a possibility.

"Hey, Johnny!" Sam was right outside her tent. "What are you doing? We're going swimming!"

"I'm coming, but I've got to get my suit back on!"

"Okay. Hurry!"

Off came his clothes. Soon he was ready. "Aren't you coming, Mom?"

"In a minute. You go on."

In case Carson was up for more play time in the lake, she decided against going swimming again. Grabbing her hairbrush and Johnny's beach towel, she left the tent and walked toward the others. Monica and Ralph waved to her. They were already in the water with the inner tube. "Come on in!"

"I just barely got out! How was the balloon ride?"

"Fantastic! You should try it before you leave the Tetons."

"Maybe I will!"

The children were clustered around Carson and Buck, who were handing out life jackets. She sat down in a camp chair, ostensibly to keep an eye on the children. But it was hard to focus when there were two tall, well-built ex-marines ready to enter the water. She finally closed her eyes and gave her damp hair a good brushing while she soaked in the heat.

THE COLOR OF Tracy's hair shimmering in the sun was indescribable. The fine strands could be real silver and gold intertwined. While the kids played with the Harrises, Carson kept his eyes above the waterline to take in the curves of her exquisitely proportioned body.

Buck emerged from the depths next to him, coughing up a storm. "I agree she's quite a sight," he whispered when he'd caught a breath. "When are you going to do something about it?"

"Is it that obvious?"

"Not to anyone but me and Ross."

"We didn't invite her family to the ranch for me to make a pass."

Buck scowled. "Hey, it's me you're talking to. I damn well know that. Tell me the truth. You haven't gotten any signals from her that she'd like you to?"

"I don't know. It's hard to read her. She's warm and friendly enough when she's with Johnny, which is most of the time."

"Maybe we need to arrange something this evening so she isn't with him. Time is fleeting. Saturday will be here before you know it."

Carson threw back his head. "Thanks for making my day, Buck."

"Just trying to help things along for a buddy."

"Sorry for snapping."

"Forget it. There's only one cure for your problem. I'll tell ghost stories in the kids' tent after everyone goes to bed. No adults allowed. While the Harrises retire to their tent, you and Tracy can sit around and talk. That ought to give you plenty of time to get creative."

"She'll probably go to her tent."

After a pause Buck said, "Like I said, get creative and follow her."

"That's been my idea since the moment we set up camp."

"Then I don't see a problem."

"I wish I didn't."

"Don't let me down, buddy. You take first watch tonight and see where it leads. Wake me up when it's my turn." Buck did a backflip away from him and swam underwater to surprise the kids.

That was easy enough for his friend to say, but Carson intended to follow through, all the same. The hourglass was emptying every second. He needed to mind his grandfather's advice when he'd been teaching Carson how to wrestle steers. "Put your fear away and seize the moment without hesitation, otherwise the opportunity is lost."

Tonight might be one of the few opportunities left to find out what was going on inside her. Armed with a plan, it helped him get through the rest of the evening.

While Carson and Buck explained why they were wearing canisters of oxygen and masks, Ralph Harris volunteered to build a small fire along the shoreline away from everyone. It would help them to avoid breathing too much smoke.

Instead of rainbow trout, they served roasted Teton hot dogs and Snake River marshmallows. The menu was a huge hit and met with Johnny's wholehearted approval.

With their meal finally over, Carson put the food away. Ralph volunteered to douse the fire and make sure there'd be no sparks. Now that it was time for bed,

Buck made his exciting announcement and the children scurried to the big tent for stories.

The Harrises eventually said good-night. Before Tracy could say the same thing, Carson told her he'd walk her to the latrine. "In case Bigfoot is lurking."

"Carson!"

He stood chuckling at a distance until she came out. "Maybe you'd better sit with me and have a soda until you're not so jumpy."

"Are you intentionally trying to frighten me?"

His pulse rate sped up. "Is it working?"

"Yes."

"That's good. I don't feel like being alone on a perfect night like this."

"It's incredible."

He liked the sound of that. They walked back to the camp in companionable silence. Carson waited for her to tell him she really was tired and needed to go to bed. Instead she sat down near him, staring out at the water.

Before dinner she'd put on a navy pullover with long sleeves over her jeans. Everything she wore suited her. Earlier, while she'd been roasting her hot dog and the flames from the fire were turning to embers, they'd cast a glow that brought out the creamy beauty of her complexion. She'd left her hair free, flowing to her shoulders. It had a lot of natural curl. He'd never met a more feminine woman.

"Tracy?"

Her gaze swerved to his. "What is it? I can tell something's on your mind."

He'd been about as subtle as a sledgehammer. "How would you like to go into Jackson with me tomorrow night?"

"You mean me and Johnny?"

"No. Just you. I want to take you dancing."

After a slight hesitation, she smiled. "I don't recall that being listed on your brochure."

He took a deep breath. Damn if it didn't always cause him to cough. "It isn't. I'm asking you out on a date, strictly off the record. If the answer's no, tell me now and we'll pretend I never brought it up."

She looked pensive. "I'm afraid I'm not a very good dancer."

Carson still hadn't been given the right answer. As far as he was concerned, this evening was definitely over. He got to his feet, too filled with disappointment to sit still. "Do I take it that's a no?"

"No!"

His heart gave a big kick at her emphatic response. "So it's a yes?"

"Yes, but let me warn you now, I'm out of practice."

"It's been a while for me, too." He studied her classic features in the near darkness. "If you remember, we listed babysitting on the brochure. Do you think Johnny could handle that?"

"I think he could, but I'd rather feel out Monica. Maybe we can trade nights. If she's willing to let Johnny stay at their cabin tomorrow night, I'll tend her children at mine the following night."

It thrilled him that Tracy was so ready with a solution. He was beginning to get the impression she wanted this date as much as he did. Otherwise, she wouldn't have agreed to go out alone with him. "Sounds like a plan that will make our little cowboys and girls happy."

A gentle laugh escaped. "Johnny really likes them."

"They're great kids." He reached for the flashlight on the table. "Plan on wearing something dressy."

"I only brought one outfit that would qualify, but I didn't think I'd wear it."

"I'll wear something a little dressier, too. Come on. It's late. I'll take you to your tent."

"I'd appreciate that." She got up and started walking. "Will you shine the light inside to make sure Bigfoot's brother isn't waiting for me?"

He smiled to himself. "I'll do that and one better. Buck and I are taking turns tonight keeping watch so everyone's safe." Once they reached her tent, he made a thorough inspection. "It's all right to go in."

As she stepped past him, their arms brushed. It was all he could do not to pull her to him.

She turned to him in the darkness. "Thank you for everything, Carson." Her voice sounded husky. "With two ex-marines guarding each other and all of us, I won't have a care in the world tonight."

He needed to get away from her *now*. "Keep the flashlight with you. If Johnny wakes up and wants you, one of us will bring him to you. See you in the morning, Tracy."

With the adrenalin pumping through him, Carson headed for the food tent and grabbed another flashlight from the box. Needing some exercise, he took a walk to check on the horses and make sure all was well.

Their little group had been making enough noise all day to scare off any bears. But on the off chance that one was hungry enough to come around and investigate, he was taking every precaution to safeguard their guests. The thought of anything happening to Tracy or

Johnny in his care was anathema to him. He'd never had such intense feelings before.

With time on his hands, he got on the phone and chatted with Ross. They talked about plans for the rest of the week. There were bookings for regular guests extending into August already. It appeared their brain-child was showing the promise of success.

This kind of news should make Carson happy. It *was* making him happy, but he had two people on his mind who were sleeping in tents very close to him. He was going out of his mind thinking about them leaving so soon and told Ross as much. That's when he heard a child's voice cry out, *"Mom—"*

It could have been any one of the three children. "Ross? One of the kids is awake. Got to go."

He took off for the bigger tent and almost ran into Buck who was holding Johnny's hand. The second the little guy saw him, he cried Carson's name and ran into his arms.

Carson got down on his haunches to hug him tight. "It's okay, Johnny. You were just having a bad dream."

"Mommy and I were at this big airport looking for you, but we couldn't find you. I kept calling for you, but you never came. Then I couldn't find my mom."

Carson looked up at Buck who'd heard everything. They'd both assumed the ghost stories had given him nightmares. Maybe they had. But Carson had featured in this one and Johnny had been looking for him.

It seemed Carson wasn't the only one hating the thought of Johnny and Tracy leaving the Tetons this coming weekend. The implication sent a shockwave through his body and wasn't lost on Buck, either.

Mercifully, the other kids stayed asleep.

"I'll take over now," Buck murmured.

Carson nodded. "Come on, Johnny. Let's go find your mom."

The boy put a trusting hand in Carson's and they walked to her tent. "Tracy?" he called to her from the opening. She stirred and sat up. "Johnny had a bad dream and wants to sleep with you."

"Oh, honey, come here." Johnny ran to her. Carson turned to leave, but Johnny's cry stopped him. "Don't go, Carson!" He sounded frantic.

"Johnny, Carson needs to go to his tent and get some sleep."

"He can sleep right here by me. Please, Mommy. I don't want him to leave."

In order to avoid a bigger disturbance he said, "Tell you what, partner. I'll stay here until you fall asleep. How's that?"

"You promise you won't go away?"

"Not until after I hear you snoring."

"I don't snore. Do I, Mom?"

She laughed softly. "Sometimes."

Tracy turned on the flashlight to find the blanket. "I'm not using this, Carson. Why don't you put this down next to Johnny." She was wearing pajamas with little footballs on them and looked adorable.

As Johnny might say, this was the funnest sleepover in the whole world.

Carson arranged the blanket into a pillow and stretched out. Their close quarters made everything cozy.

Tracy kissed her boy who'd climbed into the sleeping bag with her. "Do you want me to leave the light on?"

"Heck, no. Carson's here."

Tears stung Carson's eyes.

Tracy turned it off. "What kind of a bad dream was it?"

Johnny told her exactly what he'd told Carson.

He heard her deep sigh. "I've had dreams where I couldn't find somebody."

"You have?"

"Me, too," Carson interjected.

"Well, we're all here now and it's time to go back to sleep."

"Mom?"

"Yes?"

"I don't want to go home."

Carson's heart skipped a beat.

"Shh. We'll talk about it in the morning."

"Promise?"

"Promise."

"I love you, Mom."

"I love *you*, honey."

"Good night, Carson. I love you, too."

Carson closed his eyes tightly. "The feeling's mutual, partner. Good night." What else could he have said that wouldn't have upset Tracy?

When he'd had thoughts earlier in the day of being in the tent with her, he never dreamed he'd end up here in the middle of the night under these circumstances. In order to prove to her he wouldn't take advantage of the situation, he waited until he could tell they were asleep, then he crept out of the tent. He found Buck sitting on one of the chairs with his legs propped on another one.

"Go to bed, Buck. I'll never sleep tonight."

"Why not, besides the obvious?"

Carson brought him up to speed. "I'm afraid this plan

of ours may be backfiring big-time. We were supposed to give them a fun vacation, but now he says he doesn't want to go home. I know you're going to say he'll get over it, but until he does, Tracy's probably going to wish she'd never come."

"Speaking of Tracy, what happened out there tonight when you two were alone?"

"I asked her to go dancing with me tomorrow night. She said yes." The "yes" came out a little louder because he had to cough.

Buck moved his legs to the ground. "You weren't really surprised, were you?"

"I don't know. Ever since she got here, I've been turned inside out."

He got to his feet and stretched. "Do you wish she hadn't come?"

"If this becomes a nightmare for her because of Johnny, then yes. I have no doubt it was his father he was looking for."

"I'm sure you're right. It's only natural. But she chose to accept our invitation. There's a risk in everything and nothing's perfect in this imperfect world. You have to know they've been having a wonderful time."

"But at what cost?"

"That's your old guilt talking, Carson. You've got to stop taking on what can't be helped."

Buck was right. "I don't know how to do that."

"It's the only flaw I find in you. See you in the morning."

Chapter Seven

"Come on, honey." Johnny was slow putting on his cowboy boots this morning. "Now that we've had breakfast, they're calling us to pack up." So far he hadn't talked about his bad dream last night. That was good, because now wasn't the time for the serious discussion with him about Carson.

Johnny reached for his cowboy hat and put it on. "Do we have to go back to the ranch today?"

"Yes." She finished putting his things in the saddlebag.

"But I like it here."

"There are a lot more fun things we're going to do. Remember what Buck said while he was cooking our pancakes? Ross is taking us on a hike over in Teton Park. We haven't been there yet."

"Why isn't Carson coming with us?"

"You know why. He has business matters to take care of today."

"I'd rather stay home and ride Goldie."

Home?

"You can ride her after dinner. Here. You carry your saddlebag and I'll bring mine."

After fastening her hair back with a clip, she opened

the tent flap and they joined everyone congregated by the horses. She could hear the men coughing. Carson's black Stetson stood out as he finished saddling Goldie. He darted her a private glance before his blue gaze fell on Johnny. He took the bag from him and attached it.

"Up you go, partner." He helped him mount and handed him the reins.

"Who's going to take down our tents and stuff?"

"Some of my ranch hands. They came yesterday to set everything up for us."

"Oh."

"Remember what to do when the other ponies crowd in," he whispered. Tracy heard that and smiled.

Johnny's face brightened. "Yup."

Carson moved to Tracy's horse, Annie, who was ready to go. In a deft move he fastened Tracy's saddlebag. While she mounted, he undid the reins and put them in her hands, giving them a little squeeze.

TRACY HAD BEEN so excited about the date he'd made with her last night, she'd had trouble getting to sleep. When he'd brought Johnny to the tent in the middle of the night, his presence had made it impossible for her to settle back down. With that squeeze just now, she felt breathless.

He mounted his horse with effortless masculine precision. "Is everyone ready?"

"I am!" Sam called out.

"How about you, Rachel?"

"I've been ready for a long time." Her comment produced chuckles from everyone, including her parents.

"Then let's move out." Carson sounded like the hero in a Western film. Johnny fell in line right behind him, followed by the other kids, then the parents. Tracy stayed in front of Buck, who brought up the rear. A wagon train without a wagon. She loved it. In fact, she loved it too much. She was as bad as Johnny.

At first when they moved through the forest, she thought it was the trees making it seem darker than usual. But she soon realized clouds had moved in over the Tetons, blotting out the sun's rays. She felt the temperature drop. The sight of clouds after so many days of sunshine came as a surprise.

She dropped back to ride alongside Buck. "We had blue sky at breakfast. I can't believe how fast the weather has changed. Do you think there's going to be a storm?"

He nodded. "This cold front has moved in with more force than I'd anticipated. If it keeps up, we may not be able to go on that hike today."

Johnny wouldn't mind that at all. But he wouldn't like it if he couldn't go riding. "In that case, it'll be a good day for the children to play in the game room. A marathon Monopoly session will keep them occupied."

He laughed. "When we were young, my brothers and I used to play it all night. It drove my parents crazy."

"Where did you grow up, Buck?"

"Colorado Springs."

"I've heard it's beautiful there."

"It is, but I've decided nothing beats this place." A cough followed.

"How long do you plan to stay here?"

He flicked her an enigmatic glance. "If our business venture bears fruit, I'll build a home here and put down roots."

"What did you do before you went into the Marines?"

Buck's eyes got a faraway look. "My dad's in the construction business. Our family didn't know anything else."

"I see."

There was so much he didn't say, she heard pain and decided not to question him further. "While I have the chance, I want to thank you for all you've done to make this trip possible for Johnny and me. This is a once-in-a-lifetime adventure that so few people will ever enjoy. We won't forget your kindness and generosity for as long as we live."

"We're glad you're having such a good time. It makes everything we've done worthwhile, believe me."

While they'd been talking, they'd come out of the trees into the sagebrush. The track widened. "I'm going to ride up to Johnny and see how he's doing."

"Go right ahead. It's been a pleasure talking to you."

"For me, too, Buck."

She spurred her horse on past the others, delighted at the sight of her son moving along so comfortably on Goldie. Before he saw her, she whipped out her phone and took some more pictures of everyone. Carson was right in front of Johnny so he got into the pictures, too, without his knowledge.

As she put her phone away, she noticed the ponies edging up on Goldie. It really was funny how they wanted to be by her. In a minute they'd reached Johnny. She couldn't wait to see what would happen.

"Hey, Carson—here they come!"

His mentor moved to the side of the track to make room for him. She watched Johnny brace himself before he cried, "Giddyup!" and kicked his heels at the same time. Goldie was a smart little girl and trotted off, leaving the others behind. Sam and Rachel looked totally surprised.

Unable to help herself, Tracy urged her horse forward so she could catch up to her son. Once abreast of him she said, "Well done, cowboy."

"Did you see that, Mom?" Excitement filled his countenance.

"I sure did."

By now, Carson had caught up on his other side. "Thanks for teaching me that trick, Carson."

"Any time, partner."

Over Johnny's hat her gaze fused with Carson's. She could tell he was proud of her son. So was she. It was one of those incredible moments. "At this point I feel like we're actors in a movie on location out West."

He grinned. "We *are* out West, but instead of the Ponderosa, our star actor, Johnny Baretta, is headed with his posse for the Teton Valley Ranch on his wonder pony, Goldie!"

Johnny giggled. "You're so funny, Carson."

Oh, Carson—you're so wonderful, it hurts.

During this halcyon moment, they all heard thunder, the kind that could put a crack in those glorious mountains in the far distance. It kept echoing up and down the valley.

"Whoa!" Johnny cried out along with the other kids.

Carson whistled. "Now that's the kind of thunder that grows hair on a man's chest." Johnny burst into uproarious laughter. It set the tone for the ride in, calming any fears the children might have had. Their host turned in the saddle. "First person to reach the corral gets a banana split for lunch!"

"Goody!"

By the time the barn came into view, sheet lightning was illuminating the dark clouds that had settled in over the area. Tracy shot Carson a glance. "I've never seen anything so spectacular."

"During a storm it gets pretty exciting around here."

Almost as exciting as he was.

The first drops of rain pelted them as they rode into the barn to dismount. Bert came out of his office and helped the children down. Buck smiled at everyone. "Looks like we got home in the nick of time."

Ralph eyed the children. "I wonder who won?"

"Carson," all three kids said in unison.

He shook his head. "You were all there right behind me. I say everyone gets a banana split."

"Hooray!"

While the men removed the saddles and bridles, Johnny walked over to Carson. "Do you think the horses got scared?" Sometimes Tracy marveled over her son's sensitivity.

"After that first clap of thunder, I think they were a little fidgety, but since we didn't show any fear, they did fine out there. Tell you what. I'm going to take everyone back to the ranch house in the Jeep. But we'll have to make two trips. Why don't you kids come with me first, because I know you're hungry."

"Whoopie!"

Tracy watched them follow Carson into the drenching rain. She walked over to Ralph and Monica. This was the perfect time to talk to them in private. "Now we're alone for a minute, I have something to ask you, but please don't worry if you don't feel it's something you want to do."

When she told them, Monica's face lit up. "We were

just going to approach you about the same thing. The kids like each other and trust you."

"Johnny thinks you guys are great, too. This is perfect. I'll babysit for you tomorrow night."

"Thank you. We're dying to go into Jackson and have a little time alone."

Tracy could relate to that. She gathered the two saddlebags while they waited for Carson's return. Tonight was going to be a special time with a very special man and she planned to enjoy it to the fullest. After she and Johnny were back in Ohio, it would be a memory she would pull out and relive when the going got tough again. But she didn't want to think about the tough part right now.

CARSON HAD ONLY seen Tracy in jeans or a bathing suit. When she opened the cabin door at seven-thirty, he was treated to a vision of a different kind. With her blond hair loose, the champagne-colored skirt and gauzy blouse looked sensational on her. Soft and dreamy. Her high-heeled sandals showed off her shapely legs.

"Carson—" Her hazel eyes played over him longer than usual. "I almost didn't recognize you in a regular suit minus the boots and hat. I don't think Johnny would, either."

"A man has to be civilized around here once in a while. Are you ready?"

"Yes," she said quietly. "I'll grab my purse and jacket."

They left the cabin and he helped her into his Altima. The storm had passed, leaving everything cooler. He loved the smell of the sage after the rain. "Is Johnny all right with this?"

"I wondered about it when I broached the subject this afternoon. When he found out he'd be staying at the Harris's cabin until I got back, he didn't exactly mind we were going somewhere without him. Of course, I had to promise I'd come and get him."

"Of course." Carson started the engine and drove off. "Since you've told me how protective he can be, I guess I wondered if he put up a fuss that I'm taking you out."

"Are you kidding? The king of the cowboys?"

Her comment removed the bands constricting his lungs. The result was another bout of coughing. "After his nightmare, I worried his father was on his mind."

"I'm sure he was, subconsciously, but he didn't mention Tony at all. In fact, he hasn't talked about him once since our arrival here. That tells me you and your friends have achieved your goal to bring our family some happiness. Today made it evident that my son has come out of his shell. Your goodness and generosity are the sole reason for that. I told Buck the same thing earlier today."

Carson had noticed the two of them talking as they'd headed back to the ranch. "And what about you, Tracy? Are you enjoying yourself?"

"You know very well that question doesn't need an answer. I could never imagine myself being with another man again. Yet I found myself saying yes when you invited me out. I thought, why not? If Johnny could get on a small plane and dive-bomb into Jackson Hole, then it was time I took a risk. That should tell you a lot."

It did, but it wasn't enough. Patience had never been Carson's strong suit. "I'm taking you to the Hermitage, a French restaurant I haven't been to since my return from Maryland. It's in the Spring Creek Ranch area, a thousand feet above the valley floor.

"The view is superb. I thought you might like a change from authentic Western and enjoy some great French food along with a live band that plays a lot of romantic French songs. On Friday night after the rodeo, I'll take you and Johnny to a fun place for Western music and line dancing. Everyone gets in on the act in their duds. He'll be in his element."

He felt her eyes on him. "Be careful, Carson. You're spoiling us too much. If you treat all the families who come here at your invitation the way you're treating me and Johnny, no one will ever want to leave."

"Can I quote you on that when the time comes?" He pulled up to the crowded restaurant and turned off the engine. Luckily he'd made reservations. Even in the semidarkness, he saw color fill her cheeks.

She looked away. "You know what I meant."

"My friends and I appreciate the compliment." Levering himself from the car, he went around to help her out. The place had been built to resemble one of those religious retreats in the French Alps. He ushered her through the heavy wooden doors. The high ceilings and huge picture windows were unexpected and provided a contemporary twist.

"Carson! I couldn't believe it when I heard you'd made a reservation." A wiry older man came rushing over to the entry and kissed him on both cheeks. "Are you on leave? I haven't seen you since your *grand-père*'s funeral."

"I've left the military, Maurice, and am back for good."

"That's the best news I've heard in a long time."

His throat swelled with emotion. "It's good to see you."

"And who is this ravishing creature?"

"Please meet Tracy Baretta, one of the guests staying at the ranch with her son. Tracy, this is Maurice Chappuis, the owner."

The restaurateur's warm brown eyes studied her for a long moment. "How do you do, Tracy."

"It's very nice to meet you."

Carson would have said more, but a coughing spell stopped him. Maurice frowned. "That doesn't sound good."

"I got it when I was overseas, but I'm not contagious, so don't worry." He glanced at Tracy. "His son Jean-Paul and I were friends back in high school. Jean-Paul was a local bull riding legend. Maurice came to all our competitions. What's he up to these days?"

"Same thing as usual. Helping me here and on the ranch. Except…he got married four months ago and they're expecting!"

"You're kidding!" Carson was truly happy for him.

Maurice crossed himself. "He's off tonight. When I tell him who walked in here, he'll be overjoyed."

"Tell him to come by the ranch and bring his wife."

"I will. Now come. Sit, sit, sit. Only the best champagne in the house for you. I don't need to tell you we serve the best coq au vin in the world, and we have a new *chanteur* performing with the band. He does wonderful Charles Aznavour renditions."

"That's why we're here." He gave Maurice another hug. Seeing him like this brought the past hurtling back. Once again his guilt took over. Jean-Paul hadn't gone away. He wasn't restless, as Carson had been. Once his rodeo days were over, he'd stayed in Jackson. He'd built a life here, helping his father. Now he had a wife.

After Maurice seated Tracy, Carson took the seat opposite her at the window with its amazing view of the valley. The wine steward came over to pour them champagne. When he was gone, she eyed her dinner companion with concern.

"Maurice is wonderful, but I can tell something's wrong." Her naturally arched brows lifted. "Memories?"

He nodded soberly. "Too many. They all came rushing in at once."

"I know the feeling. When you handed that photograph to Johnny at the airport, and I saw Tony, it was like instant immersion into a former life."

"Immersion's a good word." He drank some champagne. "Mmm. You should try this. It's like velvet."

But she remained still. "You loved your grandfather, didn't you?"

"Yes."

"Then why do I sense so much sadness?"

"You know the old saying, act in haste and repent at leisure? That's me. But I don't want to talk about me tonight." He lifted his wineglass. "I'm dining with a beautiful woman and don't want anything to spoil it. Here's to an unforgettable evening."

She lifted her glass to touch his, and then sipped. "Oh—" She smiled. "That's really good."

"Isn't it?"

The waiter brought their meal and a basket of freshly baked croissants. Maurice didn't usually serve these with dinner, but he knew how much Carson loved them.

"You have to try one of these. They literally melt

in your mouth. I've eaten a dozen of them in one sitting before."

She took a bite. "I believe you."

While they ate their meal, he saw the dance band assemble across the room. A man in a turtleneck and jacket took over the mic. "Ladies and gentlemen," he said in heavily accented French. "I've been told we have a very special guest in the restaurant tonight. Monsieur Lundgren, it is up to you to choose our first number before the dancing starts."

Carson chuckled. Trust Maurice to pull this. He glanced at Tracy, whose smile haunted him. "Go on. I'm curious to know what you pick."

"How about, 'Yesterday When I Was Young'?"

Many people in the restaurant clapped because they knew the song, too. Once the man started to sing, Carson's eyes slid to Tracy's. Their eyes didn't leave each other until the singing was over.

"I first heard that song before I was sent to the hospital," he told her. "Remember the opening lines about being young and the taste of life sweet on the tongue, of treating life as if it were a foolish game?" She nodded. "All of it burned through me like a red-hot poker. That's what I'd done, and now that time was gone.

"I looked back at my own life, knowing I could never return to those times. I felt older than my grandfather who'd passed away. Opportunities had been missed. Too late I learned that the *now* of life is the essence."

Her eyes filled and she reached across the table to squeeze his hand gently.

"Let's dance." Carson stood, and reached for her to join him.

They gravitated to each other on the dance floor.

When he pulled her into his arms she whispered, "You're still young, Carson."

He drew her tighter against him without saying anything. They danced every dance. He forgot the time, the place. Carson needed the warmth of her lissome body. With each movement he inhaled her sweet fragrance and felt every breath she took.

"I need to be alone with you, Tracy. Let's get out of here." He felt a tremor shake her body as he led her back to the table. Once he'd left some bills, he ushered her out of the restaurant to the car.

A few residue clouds obscured the moon. Except for his coughing, they drove back to the ranch in silence. It was after eleven, but there was no way this evening was over. Maybe she wouldn't like it, but he pulled around to the rear of the ranch house and shut off the engine.

"This is my home. I'd like you to see how I live. I want you to come in and be with me for a while. If that doesn't—"

"It's what I'd like, too," she broke in. He sensed she wanted to be with him. What surprised him was how forthright she was. That's the way the whole night had gone.

He got out and went around to help her from the car. "The guys live upstairs. I have the back of the house to myself."

They walked down the hall to his bedroom, where Buck had done some remodeling for him. His grandfather's former room had been turned into a suite with its own sitting room and bathroom, but Carson wasn't thinking about that right now. He started to help her off with her jacket, but the moment he touched her, he couldn't help kissing the side of her neck.

"So help me, I promised myself I wouldn't do this, but I don't seem to have any control when I get close to you."

She twisted around until she faced him. That beautiful face. "Neither do I."

"Tracy—"

Carson lowered his head and covered her mouth with his own, exultant that at last he was tasting her. The singing line of her mouth had been tempting him for days. By some miracle she was kissing him back and she went on giving kiss after kiss. Like their dancing, they couldn't stop. It felt too wonderful to love this way.

He'd been empty for too many years. He wanted to go slow, but he didn't know how. She wasn't helping him. This merging of lips and bodies was so powerful, their desire for each other took on a life of its own. Carson didn't remember picking her up and carrying her to the bed. But there she was, lying on the mattress, looking up at him with a longing he could hardly credit was for him.

After crushing her mouth once more, he lifted his head, but he was out of breath. "I brought you here to… to do this…and to talk."

"I know," she half moaned. "That's why I came. We *have* to talk."

"How are we supposed to do that now? Do you have any idea how much I want to make love to you?"

"That makes two of us." Her voice trembled. "Don't hate me too much if I confess that I wanted you to kiss me to see if what I was feeling was real."

"You mean I was an experiment."

"Yes. But so was I to you—be honest about that." Her eyes beseeched him to understand. "After Tony, I—"

"You don't need to explain anything to me," he cut in. "I've been wondering about that, too, but no longer. It's real, all right." He buried his face in her fragrant hair.

"What's happened to us proves there's life after death. Until I met you, I didn't believe it. Oh, Carson." She covered his face with kisses.

HE FOUND HER mouth again, starving for her. "Now we *have* to believe it, because it's evident we're both hungry for each other. There's been an awareness between us from the first instant. Whether it's an infatuation that will burn out, only time will tell, but at least we can admit to what we're feeling right now and go on from here."

A tortured look entered her eyes. "We can't go on. This has to end tonight and you know it."

"Tonight?"

He rolled her on top of him, searching the depths of her eyes. "We've only just begun and we have three more precious days and nights together. How can you say it has to end now? How do we do that, Tracy?"

"Because we can't afford to start something we can't finish."

"Who says we can't?" he cried fiercely. "It already started Friday evening. Don't you know I don't ever want you to go home? You can't! Not when we feel this way about each other. For two people to connect the way we have is so rare, we have to hold on to it and nurture it. If I've learned nothing else, that's what war has taught me. Can you deny it?"

"Carson!" she said in genuine shock. "I couldn't possibly stay."

"That's because you're afraid."

"All right, yes. I am, for too many reasons to mention!"

"So am I. Petrified. This is new for me, too."

"We've only known each other a few days."

"That's the whole point, isn't it? How can we really get to know each other unless you stay? In order to give us a chance, I'd like you and Johnny to live in the cabin for as long as you want, until Christmas, even. That way you'll have seen all the seasons come and go except spring—which is enchanting. With weather like ours, it's important you experience it. By then, we'll know if you're ready to pack your bags or not."

She knew the "or not" meant he was talking about marriage, but he didn't say it in order not to scare her over something she wasn't ready for yet. With her, it would have to be all or nothing. He'd marry her in the morning, but he was going to give her plenty of time to get used to the idea.

Carson groaned when she started to ease herself away from him. He reached for her, but she slid to the edge of the bed and stood up. "If it were just me, I might consider staying on in Jackson at a motel for another week to see more of you. But we're talking about Johnny, too."

He got to his feet. "Exactly. He needs time to get to know the real me and see if he likes the man who's not just a cowboy. He's told me several times he doesn't want to go home. Whether he really meant it or not, he said it, and that's a start in the right direction."

She shook her head. "It just wouldn't work."

"Of course it would. We need to see where this leads."

"It might lead nowhere!" she exclaimed. "You could end up not liking me. We might find out we're not good for each other."

"Johnny may end up despising me, and you may discover you're bored and hate this lifestyle," Carson agreed. "But that's the risk we'll have to take because a fire's been lit, Tracy, and you can't ignore it."

"I'm not. I'm only trying to think with my head and not with emotions or hormones."

"That would be impossible. They all work together. I know we have to head for the Harrises' cabin, but before we walk out of here, I want you to think hard about something." He grasped her upper arms. "Will you listen?"

"Of course."

"I let my grandfather down when he was alive, but now that I'm back, I intend to keep this ranch going for my own sake as well as to honor him. The only way you and I can be together is for you to come to me. If you let fear take over, you'll be throwing away something precious. Are you willing to take that chance?"

"You make it all sound so easy, but it isn't. For one thing, I have my career."

He folded his arms so he wouldn't crush her in his arms again. "The Teton School District would welcome credentials like yours. Johnny could attend any one of six elementary schools. He'll make friends there and with the neighbors. We're only fifteen minutes away from town."

"Carson, I couldn't just stay on your property for six months."

"Then pay me rent like you do your landlord in Sandusky."

"But you built these cabins for tourists. Johnny and I would be taking up one of them. It wouldn't be fair to you and your friends after all the work you've done to make this into a dude ranch."

"I've already contacted the architect to build another one." The house of glass near the river.

"Your friends will hardly welcome the news that the family you invited here has decided to stay on. You three have started a new business together and don't need that complication."

He grimaced. "I'd hardly call you a complication, Tracy. But I know why you're throwing up all these excuses. For you to stay here will cause a major earthquake in the Baretta family. Don't bother to deny it, because I know it's true."

"They'd have a difficult time if Johnny weren't there."

"Your family could come out here for visits. They'd always be welcome."

"They're very set in their ways and don't travel often."

"What's really wrong that you're not telling me?"

She lowered her head. "They wouldn't approve."

"I get it," he fired back. "But their son has been laid to rest and their daughter-in-law has the right to get on with her life the way she sees best."

"You don't know what they're like." She raised anxious eyes to him. "My in-laws are good Catholics."

An angry laugh escaped his lips. "What would they prefer? That I fly home with you and assure them that while you're staying on my ranch, you won't be living in sin with me?"

The second she blanched, he realized his mistake

and gathered her into his arms where she fit against his as if she'd been made for him. Rocking her back and forth he whispered, "Forgive me for saying that. Already you're seeing a side of me that probably makes you glad you're leaving on Saturday. I know I sound desperate. It's because I am."

Carson found her mouth and drank deeply. He would have gone on kissing her indefinitely, but he had to cough. After it subsided he said, "Have I told you what a wonderful son you have? Last night he wanted me to stay in your tent. You have no idea what that meant to me." He lowered his mouth to kiss her again and tasted salt from her tears.

In the next instant she put her hands on his chest to stop him. "We can't do this, Carson. It's midnight. We have to go for Johnny."

He drew in his breath. "I know, but I have to have one more of these." Cupping her face in his hands, he savored another heart-stopping kiss from her lips. Her response told him things she wasn't ready to admit yet. Carson needed to be able to do this for the rest of their lives. In his gut, he knew that if she didn't end up being his wife there would be other women to provide a distraction, but he'd never marry one of them.

Ross had put it into words while they were working on the cabins in April. "You're probably one of those 'one woman' men you hear about. My great-grandfather was exactly like that. A crusty bachelor who came out to Texas from the East to find oil and make his fortune. Big business and politics were the only things on his mind.

"According to the story, he saw my great-grandmother picking bluebonnets in a field. She looked like a vision and he presented himself to her. It was history from there."

Carson had experienced a similar vision when Tracy had walked into the airline terminal. He was ready to make his own history, but he needed this woman and her son for it to happen. They made him want to be a better person because they were life to him.

Chapter Eight

"Mom? My stomach hurts."

Tracy turned in the bed to look at Johnny, who was still under his covers. Normally he was up by this time, shooting off his cap gun. "You look pale. What kind of treats did you eat last night?"

"Sam's mom made popcorn."

"Is that all you ate?"

"No. When she put me in the bedroom with Sam, he had a bag of mini chocolate bars and we ate some."

"I bet his mother didn't know about those."

"She didn't. He told me we had to keep it a secret."

"So how many did you really eat?"

"All of them."

"No wonder you're sick. Do you think you're going to throw up?"

"Yes."

She pushed the covers aside and jumped out of bed. He started running and beat her to the bathroom in time to empty his stomach. Tracy waited till he was through, then she helped him wash out his mouth.

"I still don't feel good."

"I'm not surprised. I want you to get back in bed."

"But Carson was going to take us all riding this

morning. Goldie will wonder where I am." He burst into tears, the first he'd shed since coming here.

Just the mention of Carson's name set her trembling. Last night the Harrises had left the cabin door unlocked. Carson had stolen in and brought Johnny out to the car. Her son had been sound asleep. When they reached her cabin, he'd put Johnny to bed and had left without touching her. For the rest of the night she'd ached for him until it turned into literal pain.

"I'll tell him you're not feeling well. Maybe by this afternoon you'll feel better and then we can go over to the corral."

"Will you tell him to come and see me?"

"Honey, he has other guests to take care of. In the meantime, we'll wait to see if you throw up again. If you don't, I'll get you some toast and there's Sprite in the fridge." The cabin had been stocked with enough snacks and fruit for her to skip breakfast in the dining room. "Would you like to lie down on the couch in the other room so you can watch a movie?"

"Okay."

Tracy took a blanket and pillow from his bed and tried to make him comfortable. She looked through the DVDs. "Do you want *The Hobbit* or Harry Potter?"

"I don't care."

That was his nausea talking. When it passed, then he'd ask her questions about her night out with Carson. She popped in the Harry Potter DVD.

"When are you going to call him?"

She glanced at her watch. It was quarter after eight. "In a little while. Let's give him time to eat his breakfast first." In truth she had no idea what time he ate. She'd phone him at nine.

"Don't tell Sam's mom what we did or she might get mad."

"She's so nice I'm sure she'll understand. I have to call her to let her know you won't be riding with her children this morning."

His eyes were closed. "Okay."

"I'll only be in the bedroom for a minute." She hurried in the other room and phoned the front desk. They put her call through.

"Monica? I'm glad I caught you. How are the children this morning?"

"That's funny you'd ask. Rachel's fine, but Sam says he's not feeling well."

"Neither is Johnny." In the next breath Tracy told her about the overload of chocolate.

"That little monkey of mine. I'm so sorry."

"You don't need to apologize, Monica. My son was equally guilty. I think they've learned their lesson. I just wanted you to know we won't be going riding this morning. Maybe not at all today."

"I agree we'll have to give riding a miss. I'll call Carson and let him know the situation."

Good idea.

Tracy wasn't ready to face him yet, not even over the phone. "Thank you, but don't think this changes our plan for me to tend your children. How about tomorrow night instead of tonight? Hopefully everyone will be well by then."

"That would be wonderful, if you're sure."

"Absolutely. I had a lovely time last night and want you and your husband to enjoy your evening, too. Why don't I treat tomorrow night like a special campout for the children? Our last one before we all have to leave the ranch. There's a bed for everyone here and we've got the couch. That way, you and Ralph don't have to come home until you want."

"Do you mean it?"

"Of course."

"You're one in a million, Tracy."

"So are you. We'll talk later."

After hanging up, Tracy padded into the other room. Johnny had fallen asleep again. That was good. Hopefully when he awakened, he'd feel a little better. She left the DVD on, hoping it might distract her.

Last night, while she'd been dancing with Carson, she'd wanted him to kiss her so badly, she couldn't wait to leave and go home with him. But what happened after that had shaken her world and she needed to talk to her sister-in-law, the only one who wouldn't judge her or the situation. Much as she wanted to phone Natalie, she couldn't. It wouldn't be fair to intrude on their vacation. Tracy needed to work this out on her own.

While she sat there brooding, she didn't feel like getting dressed yet. Instead she walked over to the table to make herself some coffee. It was something to do while her son slept on. Among the snacks she found a granola bar. While she ate, she sat down at the table to watch the movie and sip the hot brew.

Though she stared at the TV screen, her thoughts were full of last night's conversation with Carson and the way he made her feel while they'd kissed each other in mindless passion.

Much as she might want a repeat of that rapture for the rest of her life, Tracy couldn't just stay on here. What he'd suggested was impossible. Once she'd met Tony, the Barettas had become her whole family. They weren't simply her in-laws. With the loss of their son, they'd clung to Tracy and she to them. She didn't know what she and Johnny would have done without them.

They'd be so hurt if she told them she'd be staying on in the Tetons for a while. Her plans to visit them in Cleveland would have to be put off until later in the summer. She couldn't do that to them, no matter how much she dreaded the thought of leaving Carson.

What he'd said was true. If there was any chance that a lasting, meaningful relationship could develop, they needed to explore those feelings. Would they be as strong as their physical attraction for each other?

The way she felt right now, she couldn't imagine that attraction ever burning out, but she knew it could happen. One of the couples she and Tony had been friends with after they'd moved to Sandusky had recently divorced. They'd seemed to be so in love.

She needed to put last night's events away. For Tracy to want to be with a man she'd only just met and who lived thousands of miles away was ludicrous. The more she thought about it, the more she realized it would be the height of selfishness to stay here. Johnny might be having the time of his life on this vacation, but he needed loving family surrounding him. She couldn't keep him away from that.

Tracy had been blessed with a loving marriage to Tony. Now it was up to her to give Johnny the life they'd envisioned for their boy. One that included his favorite cousin, Cory, plus his other cousins, loving aunts and uncles, adoring grandparents. Good friends from the neighborhood and school would come with time.

From the deep fathoms of her troubling thoughts, she heard a knock on the door. Maybe it was Rachel with a message from Sam. Afraid it might wake up Johnny, she padded over to the door in her Cleveland Browns pajamas and opened it.

Bright blue eyes greeted her. "Dr. Lundgren at your service, Mrs. Baretta. My receptionist informed me I needed to make a house call on a new patient. She tells me he overdosed on Kisses. I can relate to that. In fact I'm still suffering the effects because I've become addicted to them."

Carson...

Heat swept through her body into her face.

"Hey—Carson?" Johnny called from the couch with excitement while she was trying to recover her breath.

"Yup. I've brought some stuff to make you feel better."

Johnny hurried to the door. He didn't look as pale as before. "What is it?"

Carson reached into the sack he carried. "Some Popsicles when you're ready for one."

"Thanks! I threw up this morning, but I'm feeling a little better now."

"That's good. Maybe you'd like to watch the DVDs I brought of Hoppy."

"Goody!"

Tracy was completely flustered, having been caught in her pajamas with her hair disheveled. "Well, aren't you a lucky boy. Thank you, Carson. Please come in. I'll get dressed and be out shortly." She flew through the cabin to her bedroom and shut the door.

When she emerged a few minutes later in jeans and a blouse, the two of them were on the couch. Johnny was sucking happily on a banana Popsicle while he told

Carson how he got sick. Tracy thought he might throw it up later, but at least he was taking in some liquid.

"A long time ago I remember eating too many Tootsie Rolls and got a stomachache for a whole day. I still can't eat one."

"I did the same thing on some fudge cookies," Tracy admitted.

Carson's gaze drifted over her. "Sounds like you're both chocolate addicts. By the way, I like the mother–son outfits."

Johnny spoke before she could. "My aunt Natalie gave these to us for Christmas. She and Cory have a pair, too. We love the Cleveland Browns."

"How about their quarterback, Colt McCoy?"

"Yeah." They high-fived each other.

"You're not going to leave are you?" Johnny cried when Carson unexpectedly got to his feet.

"Nope. I was going to put in one of the DVDs for you to watch."

"Good. I don't want you to go. Mom said you had a lot of other stuff to do today."

He walked over to the player. Glancing at them over his shoulder he said, "I was planning on taking you guys riding, but since that's out, I thought I'd hang out with you till you're feeling better."

"I probably won't be better all day." Her son was milking this for all it was worth.

Tracy didn't dare look at Carson or she'd burst out laughing. Instead she reached for an apple and sat down in the chair, putting her legs beneath her. In seconds he'd exchanged the DVDs in the player, and one of the old cowboy movies with the kind of music written for the early Westerns came on the screen.

"William Boyd," she said aloud. Seeing the actor's name brought back memories of the past with her parents.

Johnny frowned. "I thought his name was Hoppy."

"That's the character he plays in the film, honey."

"Oh."

"I wonder if Lucky is as cute as I remember," she teased. A little imp of mischief prompted her to see if she could get a rise out of Carson.

She wasn't disappointed when his gaze narrowed on her. "Why don't we take a vote at the end of the show?"

The by-play passed over Johnny. He moved his pillow so he could lie against Carson's leg. It was exactly the kind of thing he would do when he watched TV with Tony and got sleepy. Tracy couldn't believe how comfortable her son was with Carson, who seemed to take all this in as the natural course of events.

Before long, Hoppy and his friends came riding into town at full speed.

"There he is, riding his horse, Topper—" Carson blurted, sounding as excited as a kid. "To me, he was the greatest superhero in the world."

Johnny sat up. "But that guy in the black cowboy hat looks like a grandfather!"

Laughter burst out of Carson so hard it brought on a coughing spasm.

Tracy's shoulders shook. "He really does look old now that you think about it, but Lucky's still as cute as ever."

"That white hat's too big on him, Mom. He looks like a nerd. What's his horse's name?"

"Zipper."

Johnny giggled. As for Carson, he had a struggle to

stop laughing. "Well, Mom, I'm afraid I have to throw in my vote with Johnny. That makes two of us who disagree with you."

"You guys are just jealous."

"How come you like Hoppy so much?" Johnny's tone was serious.

She watched Carson's features sober. "I don't remember my dad. When I saw Hoppy's films, I imagined my dad being like him. A great cowboy who was really good, really courageous and always fair. My grandpa was like that, too. I was lucky to be raised by him."

"Yeah," Johnny murmured.

"You know something? You were lucky to have your father for as long as you did."

"I know."

"And now you have your grandfather."

"Yup. He's awesome. Carson? Do you miss your grandpa?"

"Yes. Very much. I bet you've missed yours this trip, too."

"Nope, 'cos he's not dead." *Shock.* "I can call him and Grandma whenever I want."

"I envy you."

Tracy felt Carson's pain. They needed to get off the subject. "You two are missing the show." She doubted anyone was really concentrating on it, but the room fell quiet until the end of the movie. When it was over, she got up to turn it off. "Are you getting hungry, Johnny?"

"No. Can I have another Popsicle?"

That was a good sign the nausea was subsiding. She picked up the paper with the sticks and threw them in the wastepaper basket, then drew another treat out of the small freezer. "Is cherry okay?"

"Yes."

He still wasn't well if this was all he could tolerate, but at least he hadn't been sick again. When she turned, she noticed Carson was already on his feet. She had a hunch he was leaving and her spirits plummeted. He looked down at Johnny.

"I hate to go, but I have to take some guests riding this afternoon. When I'm through, I'll phone to find out if you're hungry. If so, I'll bring you and your mom some dinner."

"I wish you didn't have to leave." He looked crestfallen to the point of tears.

"Can you thank him for the Popsicles and the movies?"

Johnny nodded. "Thanks, Carson."

"You're welcome." He flicked a glance to Tracy. "I'll have one of the kitchen staff bring you lunch."

"You don't have to do that. There's plenty to eat here."

"I want to do it," he insisted. "Does a club sandwich sound good?"

"Wonderful."

"Great. I'll have her bring some soda crackers, too."

There wasn't anything Carson couldn't, wouldn't or didn't do. *He* was the superhero.

After he left, gloom settled over the cabin. Johnny lay there watching cartoons while she tried to interest herself in the book she'd brought. Except for the arrival of her lunch, it turned out to be the longest day either of them had lived through in a long time.

On a happier note, by midafternoon Johnny was hungry enough to eat the crackers and drink some Sprite. Things were improving. Though neither of them said it, they were both living for the evening when Carson had promised to come back.

When he finally arrived, he brought them country-fried steak and the trimmings, plus chicken-noodle soup and toast for Johnny. The sight of him walking through the cabin door dressed in a black crew neck shirt and jeans changed the rhythm of her heart.

He'd also brought a colorful puzzle of all the planets. Johnny adored it and they worked on it until his head drooped. Tracy had been counting the minutes until she could put him into bed. The thought of being alone at last with Carson was the only thing driving her.

WITH A HEART thudding out of control, Carson sat on the couch, waiting for her. When she appeared he whispered, "Come over here."

Tracy moved toward him. He caught hold of her hand and pulled her down so she lay in his arms. The fragrance of her strawberry shampoo seduced him almost as much as the feel of her warm body cuddled up to his.

A deep sigh escaped his lips as they swept over each feature of her face. "I've been dreaming about being with you like this since you first arrived. After last night, it's a miracle I functioned at all today. You're a beautiful creature, Tracy."

She smiled. "Men always say that about a woman, but the well-kept secret is that every woman knows there's nothing more beautiful than a man who possesses all the right attributes. *You,* Carson Lundgren, were given an unfair number of them."

"As long as you think that, I'll never complain." Unable to stand it any longer, he started to devour her mouth with slow, deliberate kisses that shook them both.

He wrapped his legs around her gorgeous limbs, needing to feel every inch of her.

She explored his arms and back with growing urgency. When her hands cupped the back of his neck to bring him even closer, he realized what a sensuous woman he held in his arms. It filled him with an ecstasy he'd never known before. This was an experience he couldn't compare to anything else.

"I want to take you to bed so badly I can hardly bear it, but this isn't the place, not with Johnny sleeping in the next room."

Tracy covered his face with kisses. "It's a good thing he's nearby, because you've done something to me. I don't think I'll ever be the same, even when I'm back in Ohio."

"If your craving is as strong as mine, then you won't be going anywhere."

"You sounded fierce just now." She gave him a teasing smile before kissing him long and hard.

He finally lifted his mouth from hers. "You know why that is. We're not playing a game." A cough came out of him. "This is for real."

"Carson—" She framed his face with her hands. "I'm trying to be as honest with you as I know how to be. As you can see, I'm completely enamored with you. I spent all night asking myself questions—why this should be, and why it would happen now.

"Tony's only been gone a year. So many things have been going through my mind. Am I feeling this because this is my first experience with another man since he died and I'm missing physical fulfillment? Is this rugged Western cowboy so different from any man I've ever known, that I'm blinded by the comparison? When the newness wears off, will he be disenchanted by my Ohio roots?"

He smoothed some silvery-gold strands off her cheek. "To be brutally honest, I've been asking the same questions, and others. Why am I taken with a woman who will keep another man in her heart forever? Why have I met a woman who has a son she'll always put first? Am I crazy to want to deal with all that, knowing she's bonded to her husband's family?"

A tortured expression broke out on her face. "The way you put it, it does sound crazy. As I told you last night, you're young with your whole life ahead of you. Some single, Western woman who's never met the right man is going to come along and knock your socks off. You'll be the only man in her heart. The two of you will start a new family together."

Carson grimaced. "As long as you're playing what-if, can you imagine the irony of another widow with a child, like yourself, coming to the ranch this summer and sweeping me off my feet? A woman with the wisdom to grab at a second chance for happiness?"

Shadows darkened her eyes. "Actually, I can. I've been haunted by that very possibility since last night."

He raised himself up. "Are you willing to risk it and fly back to Ohio on Saturday, away from me? Before you find out what joy you might be depriving the three of us of?"

She shook her head. "You don't know Johnny. This trip represents a huge change for him.

"In the heat of the moment he'd agree to do whatever I wanted, but in time his true feelings will surface. When they do, it could be traumatic for him if he wants to go home because he misses the family too much, but feels guilty because he doesn't want to hurt your feelings.

"I don't question his affection for you, Carson. But he'll feel the pull of family the longer he's out here. I'd rather spare him that kind of pain."

Her words gutted him. He got up from the couch, unconsciously raking a hand through his hair. "You know your son the way I never will. I have no say when it comes to your mother's intuition. It's clear to me you've made up your mind. Have no fear I'll try to persuade you further."

Tracy looked wounded as she slid off the couch. "You know I'm right," her voice trembled.

He wheeled around. "No. I don't know that. What I do know is that when you leave, you'll be preventing us from learning the truth. For the rest of our lives we'll have that question mark hanging over us. But as we've discovered by surviving the war, life goes on."

"Carson," she pleaded.

"Carson what? You've said it all, Tracy. Now I've got to go. If Johnny feels well in the morning, bring him to the barn after breakfast. I'm driving the kids to the upper pasture. My foreman has been in touch with some other ranchers and has found a cow with a blue-eyed calf for me. I'd like one of the kids to find it."

Tears glistened in her eyes. "They'll be overjoyed."

"I still need to come up with a prize. Do you think a pair of chaps?"

She wiped the tears away with the heel of her hand. "You already know the answer to that question."

He tried to ignore her emotion. "After lunch, I'll take them horseback riding. As for Friday, I'll be doing some ranching business during the day, but Ross or Buck will take them riding for the last time. I'm still good to drive them to the rodeo on Friday evening."

"Johnny's living for it," she whispered.

"I think he'll enjoy it. On Saturday morning, I'll be running you and the Harrises to the airport in the van. With the children leaving at the same time, it should make things easier all the way around. I expect I'll see you in the morning."

Carson started for the door, but saw movement in his peripheral vision. "Don't come any closer." *Not ever again.*

He left the cabin, suppressing a cough until he got outside. When it subsided, he climbed in the Jeep without looking back. En route to Jackson, he phoned Ross and told him he was going into town in case anyone needed him.

"You sound like hell."

"That's where I am."

"If you want company, I'll tell Buck I'm joining you."

"Thanks, Ross, but I'm not fit to be around anyone."

"Tracy's still leaving on Saturday?"

"Yup."

"Sorry, bud."

"I'll live, unfortunately."

Carson hung up and continued driving to Jackson where he headed for the Aspen Cemetery. The small resting place was closed at sunset, but that didn't stop him. He pulled off the road and hopped a fence. His parents and grandparents were buried in the same plot up on the hillside near some evergreens. This was the first time he'd been here since the funeral.

The moon had come up and illuminated the double headstones. In a few strides he reached them and hunkered down to read the names and dates. *Beloved Son and Daughter* was inscribed on his parents' granite stone. It had been here for twenty-eight years. How many times had Carson come to this sacred place as a youth to talk to them?

For his grandparents, he'd had the words inscribed, *Our Last Ride Will Be to Heaven.* Carson had heard his grandfather say it often enough while he was alive. He could hear him saying it now and wept.

Finally, blinking back the tears, his gaze fell on the grassy spot next to it. One day it would be Carson's own grave. When someone buried him here, there'd only be a single headstone. That would be the end of the Lundgren line.

"Sorry, Grandpa. I finally met that woman you were asking me about. But like everything else important that happened in my life, I got there too late. Marriage isn't in my destiny. But I swear I'll take care of the ranch so you're not disappointed in me."

If the guys were still in business with him when the end came, he had no doubt they'd be married with families. He'd deed them the title and their families could carry on the Lundgren legacy. They been brought together at a low ebb in their lives and had formed an unbreakable bond.

But if it turned out they wanted and needed to go back to their former lives after this experiment was over, he'd will the property to the Chappuis family. Maurice had been like a surrogate uncle to him. Jean-Paul had been his best friend in his early days. Carson couldn't think of anyone he'd want more to inherit. No family had ever worked harder to carve out a life here. Either way, the ranch would be in the best of hands.

Having made his peace, he returned to the ranch. Two more days and she'd be gone. He would have to play the congenial host to Johnny without the boy knowing Carson's pain. The whole point of inviting their family here in the first place was to bring a little happiness into their lives. To that end he was still fully committed.

Chapter Nine

"I found one!"

From her perch on a hay bale, Tracy heard Sam's shout of delight. The calf with the blue eyes had been discovered.

Carson praised everyone for looking, but Sam was proclaimed the winner. In a few minutes Johnny came running through the herd to the truck. He'd recovered from his stomach upset but was now afflicted with another problem. When she pulled him into the truck bed, he was fighting tears.

"What's wrong, honey?" As if she didn't know.

"I wanted to find it."

"I know, but so did Rachel."

"Carson's going to give him a pair of chaps."

"Think how happy it will make him."

"But I wanted to be the one so he'd be proud of me." He broke down and flung himself at her.

With that last remark, her heart ached for him. "He's always proud of you. You know what I think? You're a little tired after being sick yesterday."

"No, I'm not."

"Then hurry and dry your eyes because everyone's coming. You don't want anyone to see how you feel.

Why don't you go over to the basket and get us both some water?"

"Okay," he muttered.

The kids came running over to the truck. Carson lifted them inside. She saw him glance at Johnny with concern, then his gaze swerved to her. It was the first time all morning he'd actually looked at her. When they'd arrived at the pasture, she'd already decided to stay put in the truck so she wouldn't have to interact with Carson any more than she had to.

When he'd left her cabin last night, she'd known he'd be keeping his distance until they left Wyoming, but this new estrangement was killing her.

Afraid he knew it, she gave Sam a hug. "Congratulations! You must have sharp eyes!"

"Yeah." He smiled. "I couldn't believe it."

"I wish I found it first," Rachel lamented.

Tracy nodded. "We all know how you feel. Better luck next time." She turned to Johnny. "Why don't you hand everyone a drink while you're at it, honey? You've all worked hard in this hot sun."

He passed the drinks around, but his face was devoid of animation.

Carson closed the tailgate. "If everyone's in, we'll head back to the ranch for lunch."

He walked around to the front, draining his water bottle. Once he'd emptied it he called out, "Catch, Johnny!" and tossed it into the back of the truck before climbing into the cab.

By some miracle her son nabbed it, causing a smile to spread on his face.

On the way back, Tracy chatted with the children about the coming sleepover. Soda was allowed, but no candy. What movie did they want to watch? What board games did they want her to choose from the game room? To her relief, Johnny started to settle down and be his friendlier self. Knowing Rachel had lost out, too, helped a little.

When Carson let them out of the back of the truck after they'd arrived in front of the ranch house, Tracy moved right with the kids and jumped down from the end before Carson could reach for her. It was a bittersweet relief to hurry inside with them, knowing he'd disappear for a while.

The kids had the routine down pat. Bathroom first, to wash their hands. As they emerged into the foyer a few minutes later, Tracy heard a familiar female voice call out, "Giovanni! Look at you in those cowboy clothes!"

Her mind reeled.

No-o.

It couldn't be.

But it was. No one else called him by their pet name for him.

"Grandma?"

"Yes! Grandma and Papa. Come and give us a hug. We've missed you so much!"

Tracy was so unprepared for this, she almost fainted. Johnny sounded equally shocked, but he ran to them. His grandmother kissed him several times, and then his grandfather picked him up and hugged him hard. Both of them were attractive and had dark hair with some silver showing. Sylvia was even wearing a pantsuit, something she rarely did.

It was painful for Tracy to watch the interaction, because conflicting emotions were swamping her. To see them here so removed from their world…

She didn't know what all had gone on to bring them to Wyoming when her vacation wasn't over yet, but she had a strong inkling.

Between Johnny's conversation with them on the phone the other day, and her conversation with Natalie, her in-laws were curious enough to get on a plane and come. It was totally unlike them.

She felt the other kids' eyes on her, needing an explanation. "Children? I'd like you to meet Johnny's grandparents from Ohio, Sylvia and Vincent Baretta. Dad and Mom? Please meet Rachel and Sam Harris from Florida. We've all become friends while we've been staying here."

"Oh, it's so nice to meet Johnny's friends," her mother-in-law said, patting their cheeks.

Her father-in-law still held Johnny while he reached for Tracy and kissed her. "After our talk with Giovanni the other morning, we decided to surprise you."

"You certainly did that." She still couldn't believe they'd come.

"Hi!" Monica had just appeared in the foyer with Ralph. "What's all the excitement?"

"These are my grandparents!" Johnny announced. "They came to see me ride Goldie!"

Okay. The pieces of the puzzle were starting to come together.

"Do you like my cowboy hat and boots? Carson took us to the store to get them."

Sylvia clapped her hands. "You look wonderful! Who's Carson?"

"He owns this whole ranch, Grandma. He rides bulls in the rodeo and is king of the cowboys!" Johnny's eyes shone like stars.

Tracy needed to do something quick. "Mom and Dad Baretta? Please meet Monica and Ralph Harris." They walked over and shook hands.

Monica smiled. "What a thrill for you, Johnny!"

"Yeah. Wait till I tell Carson! Let's hurry and eat. I'll take you over to the corral after lunch. He takes us riding every day! This morning he drove us to the pasture!"

"And guess what?" Rachel looked at her parents. "Sam found the blue-eyed calf."

"Yes, and Carson's going to give me a brand new pair of chaps to take home for winning."

"Good for you." Ralph patted his son on the back.

"We don't want to go home," Sam told his parents. "Carson told us about all these neat hikes we can go on in the Tetons. We just barely got here."

"I don't want to go home, either." Johnny took up the mantra. "Carson said the ponies will miss us. We can't leave them, Mom!"

Tracy heard her mother-in-law give the nervous little laugh she sometimes made when she didn't quite know what was going on. Johnny's grandfather lowered him to the floor. Still reeling, she said, "Why don't we go in the dining room for lunch, and then we can talk."

The room was fairly crowded. Tracy found two tables close together. While the Harrises took one of them, she guided her in-laws to the other. Johnny sat down between his grandparents, talking a mile a minute. Carson this and Carson that.

After their waitress took the orders, Tracy was finally able to ask a few questions. "When did you get here?"

Vincent had been quiet most of the time. "We flew

into Salt Lake from Cleveland, then caught a flight to Jackson last evening and stayed at a motel. Today we rented a car and drove over here to surprise you."

"Well, it's wonderful to see you." Her voice trembled. It really was, but she was still incredulous.

"These mountains are overpowering!" Sylvia exclaimed. "It's beautiful here, but I can tell we're in a much higher altitude."

"I love it here!" Johnny blurted. "It's my favorite place in the whole world."

Tracy saw a look of surprise in her in-laws' eyes. She had an idea they, too, were in shock over the change in their formerly withdrawn grandson. Suddenly Johnny jumped up from the table.

"Hey, Carson—" He ran over to the tall cowboy in the black Stetson and plaid shirt walking toward them and hugged him around the waist. "My grandma and grandpa came to see me. Will you take us all riding?"

"Sure I will," Tracy heard him say as if it were the most normal thing in the world that her in-laws had shown up unannounced and uninvited.

Johnny made the introductions. Vincent stood up to shake Carson's hand. "It was a great thing you and your fellow marines did, inviting Tracy and Giovanni here, Mr. Lundgren. Thank you for honoring our son this way. We're very grateful to you for showing our grandson such a good time."

"We certainly are," Sylvia chimed in.

"The honor has been all ours, Mr. and Mrs. Baretta. I'd be happy to introduce you to my business partners, but they're both out with other guests at the moment. It pleases me to tell you that Johnny has turned into quite a horseman already." He coughed. "I'll be over at the corral when you want to see him ride."

"We'll be right over after we eat."

"Please feel free to use all the facilities while you're here."

"That's very generous of you. Sylvia and I are staying in Jackson. We decided we'd join our family and take them to Yellowstone Park before we fly back home together. It will be a new adventure for all of us."

A gasp escaped Tracy's throat, causing Carson to glance at her briefly, but she couldn't read anything in those blue slits. Johnny hurried over to Tracy. He put his lips against her ear. "I don't want to go to Yellowstone."

"We'll talk about this later," she murmured. "Sit down and eat your lunch."

Carson tipped his hat, and then stopped at the Harrises' table to talk to them for a minute before he left the dining room in a few long, swift strides. Tracy's heart dropped to her feet. A subdued Johnny sat down, but he only played with his hamburger.

Sylvia patted his hand. "We got a suite with another room so you can stay with us tonight."

"We can't, Grandma. We're having a sleepover at our cabin with Rachel and Sam." This time Tracy saw definite hurt in Sylvia's eyes. Vincent's face had closed up.

"I'm afraid I promised Monica and Ralph," Tracy explained.

"They babysat me while Mom and Carson went out to dinner." Johnny was a veritable encyclopedia of information, but every word that came out of his mouth caused his grandparents grief.

"Well then, we'll have to do it on Friday night."

"But Carson's taking us to the rodeo!"

Tracy needed to put a stop to this, but didn't know how. "When are you flying back?"

"Tuesday," Vincent informed her. "If you call the airline, you can change your flight so we can all fly home together."

Johnny slumped down in his seat. "I don't want to go home."

Though she couldn't condone his behavior, she understood it. "Mom and Dad?" They looked hurt and confused. "If you'll excuse us, we'll meet you at the corral. Drive your car over to the barn. You can't miss it and we'll be waiting for you. Come on, Johnny."

He bolted out of his chair without giving his grandparents a kiss and ran over to the other kids. It wounded her for their sake, but the damage was done now. Soon the three children preceded Tracy out of the dining room. She needed a talk with her son, but this wasn't the time.

Tracy saw Carson's Jeep outside the barn before they reached the corral. Bert had already saddled the ponies. Carson came out leading Annie and Blueberry.

Tracy stood at the fence. While the children waited for Bert to help them mount, she watched Carson help Johnny. The play of male muscles in his arms and across his back held her mesmerized.

She heard the sound of a car and turned in time to see her in-laws get out and walk over to her. "You're in for a treat," she promised them. "We've done a lot of riding."

"Watch me!" Johnny called out to his grandparents.

All three children rode well, but Johnny stole the show as he walked Goldie around the corral like an old hand. She saw the pride in her in-laws' eyes. "You look wonderful!" they both called out to him. Vincent had tears in his eyes.

Johnny's face was beaming. "She's *my* pony."

"She's beautiful," Sylvia cried.

"Come on and ride, Grandpa. Carson's going to take us down to the Snake River and back."

"Why don't you go?" Tracy urged him. "You can ride the horse I've been riding. Sylvia and I will stay here until you get back." This would be a good time to feel out her mother-in-law over their unexpected arrival.

Johnny's invitation must have put Vincent in a better mood because he said, "I think I will."

"What about you, Sylvia? Maybe you'd like to ride, too?"

"Not me. You go ahead, Vincent. Tracy and I will have a good visit while you're gone."

It sounded like Sylvia wanted to talk to Tracy in private. They'd had a definite agenda in coming out here. Vincent was curious about the man who'd caused this change in his grandson. This would give him a chance to get a feel for him. They'd probably talk about the war and the circumstances leading up to Tony's death.

As for Carson, a picture was worth more than a thousands words of explanation from her. During the ride with Vincent, he'd come to know and understand better the dynamics that made up the Baretta family. He'd already learned a lot from their surprise visit.

The two men spoke for a minute before Vincent climbed in the saddle. He'd ridden horses in parades with the other firefighters and looked good up there. He always did, especially when he had to dress in his formal uniform. She realized Tony would have looked a lot like him if he'd had the opportunity to live a full life.

Oddly enough, that sharp pain at the remembrance of her husband was missing. The only pain she was feeling right now was a deep, soul-wrenching kind of pain as she watched the king of the cowboys mount his horse with effortless grace. From beneath the brim of his hat, he shot Tracy a piercing glance. "We'll be gone a couple of hours. I'll bring everyone back in the Jeep."

She took a deep breath. "We'll be waiting."

On that note he nodded and led everyone out of the corral, away from her.

This is what you wanted, Tracy, so why the anguish? Except that it wasn't what she wanted. She'd been looking forward to the ride this afternoon with each breath she took. Every second with Carson was precious until they had to leave.

When she couldn't see them anymore for the tears she was fighting, she walked toward the car. "Come on, Sylvia. I'll drive us back to our cabin and fix you a cup of coffee." Her mother-in-law was a big coffee drinker.

"I like the sound of that." Sylvia handed her the keys. "This is very beautiful country," she said as they drove through the sage. "When we saw the brochure on the internet, I couldn't appreciate it the way I do now."

"You have to be here and see those Tetons to realize the grandeur."

"You love it here as much as Johnny does, don't you?"

With that serious inflection in Sylvia's voice, it was the kind of question that deserved a totally honest answer. "Yes."

Tracy pulled the car up to the cabin and they went inside. "The bathroom is through there, Sylvia. While you freshen up, I'll fix us some coffee." Her mother-in-law liked it with cream and sugar. Tracy added a few snacks to a tray and put it on the coffee table.

A few minutes later they were both ensconced on the couch. "This is a very charming cabin, sunny. So was the dining room at the ranch house. You say this whole ranch belongs to Mr. Lundgren?"

Instead of the usual chitchat about family, Sylvia had zeroed in on Carson. Tracy couldn't say she was surprised. "Yes. The Teton Valley Ranch has been in their family since the early 1900s. His grandparents raised him here after his parents were killed. Carson's grandfather died recently and left him everything."

"Johnny told us he isn't married. He's certainly young to have so much responsibility."

Oh, Sylvia... "There's no one more capable."

"Obviously. Why does he cough so much?"

Tracy explained about him and his friends who'd met at Walter Reed. "Because of their illness, they were discharged from the military and decided to make this place into a dude ranch.

"Next month, another family they're honoring will be arriving. The plan is to take care of several more war widows with children by the time summer is over. They're quite remarkable men."

"I agree."

Tracy moistened her lips nervously. "Sylvia, why didn't you let me know you were coming?"

"I wanted to, but Vincent felt it would be more fun to surprise you. You know how much he loves Johnny. Every time he looks at him, he sees Tony. It was hard for him to see you two leave on this trip."

"And hard for you, too, I bet," Tracy added.

Sylvia teared up. "Yes, but I was glad for you to have

this opportunity and told him. He was morose after you left. It came as a shock to hear Johnny talk about this man over the phone. He didn't mention his father once."

I know.

"That upset Vincent so much, especially after we'd heard Natalie telling Sally about this exciting cowboy you met. After we got off the phone with Johnny, Vincent called to make reservations to fly out here."

It was exactly as Tracy had thought. Her father-in-law had felt threatened.

"Don't be upset with Vincent, Tracy. He's different since Tony died, because he doesn't want anything to change. He wants to be there for you and Johnny."

"I know that, Sylvia, and I love him for it."

"But you didn't like our coming here out of the blue. If you could have seen your face." She reached over to squeeze Tracy's hand. "I don't need to ask what this man means to Johnny. What I want to know is, how much does he mean to you?"

Tracy's heart was thudding so hard, she had to get up from the couch. "I— It's hard to put into words," her voice faltered.

"That means it's serious."

She wheeled around. "It could be," she answered with all the truth in her, "but I don't mean to hurt you or Dad. You know Tony was my life."

"Hey—you forget I'm a woman, too." She got to her feet. "Our son has been dead for a year. I have eyes in my head. When this tall, blue-eyed god walked toward our table in the dining room, he made *my* heart leap."

"Oh, Sylvia—" Tracy reached out and hugged her mother-in-law. She'd never loved her more than at this moment. For a few minutes they both cried. Finally

Tracy pulled away and wiped her eyes. "He's asked me to stay on so we can really get to know each other."

"Does Johnny know this?"

"No, and I don't want him to know." Having broken down this far, Tracy decided to tell Sylvia everything and ended up admitting all her reservations. "After losing Tony, if it didn't work out, Johnny could be severely damaged. I told Carson it wouldn't work and that's the way we've left it."

"If, if—" Sylvia exclaimed dramatically. "You can't worry about the ifs! Do you remember Frankie, who was killed two years ago battling that warehouse fire?"

"Yes. It was horrible."

"No one thought his wife and daughters would get over it. One of the other firefighters looked out for her, and six months later they were married and expecting a baby of their own. These things happen and they should! What if she'd said she couldn't risk it? Now she has a father for her girls and a new baby with this man she loves."

Tracy was struggling. "How do you think Frankie's parents felt about it?"

"At first they had a hard time. Now they're fine with it."

She looked at Sylvia. "Can you honestly see Vincent being fine with this? Carson's not a firefighter. His life is here, running this ranch. If I were to get to know him better, Johnny and I would have to stay out here, otherwise a relationship wouldn't be possible."

Sylvia's brows lifted. "You worry too much. Yes, Vincent is having difficulty letting go, but this situation isn't about your father-in-law or me. You let *me* worry about him. This is about *your* life and Johnny's, what's best for the two of you. In time you'll get your answer."

"You're the wisest woman I know. I love you, Sylvia."

"I love you, too. I always will. Since neither Vincent nor I have ever been to Yellowstone, he has his heart set on taking Johnny to see the Old Faithful geyser. Why don't we all leave for the park after the rodeo? He has us booked at Grant Village. That will give us Saturday, Sunday and Monday together. Then we'll drive you back here to the ranch and leave Tuesday. Perhaps by then you'll know your mind better."

It was a good plan. Three days with his grandparents, and Johnny might realize he was ready to go home to Ohio, especially when he remembered Sam and Rachel would be gone. Three days away from Carson would give Tracy some perspective, too. At the moment she had none.

"WILL YOU COME to our sleepover?"

Carson smiled at Johnny as he helped him off his pony. "I'll do better than that. I'll bring pizza for your going-away party."

Johnny frowned. "What do you mean?"

"You're leaving for Yellowstone after the rodeo, so I thought we'd celebrate tonight."

"But we'll be back."

"I don't know what your mother's plans are, Johnny." Out of the corner of his eye, he watched his grandfather dismount. Carson hated to admit it, but he was a good man who obviously adored his grandson and couldn't wait to get him home to Ohio.

Carson's gut twisted when he thought back to his

conversation with Tracy, who loved her in-laws. Their hold on her and Johnny was fairly absolute. "I'll bring enough for your grandparents, too." He turned to the others. "Let's get you guys home so you can get ready for the pizza party."

"Yay!" the others cried, but not Johnny.

Everyone got in the Jeep and they took off. He dropped Sam and Rachel at their cabin, and then headed for Tracy's. The rental car was out in front. She'd been there all afternoon with her mother-in-law. It was no accident her in-laws had decided to show up. She'd been right about Tony's family. They were very protective. *You don't have a chance in hell, Lundgren.*

Mr. Baretta sat next to Carson. When he stopped the truck, the older man turned to him. "It's been a privilege to go riding with you. I can see Johnny has been in the best of hands." He shook Carson's hand and got out to help his grandson.

Since he couldn't handle seeing Tracy right now, Carson went straight to the ranch house without looking back. He made a beeline for the kitchen and put in an order for pizza for six. While he was at it, he'd bring the chaps for Sam.

He saw Ross and Buck in the office. "I'm glad you're both here." He walked inside and shut the door.

Ross eyed him curiously. "The Harrises told us Johnny's grandparents showed up."

"You heard right."

"That's interesting," Buck muttered on a cough. "What's going on?"

"They've missed Johnny and came to get him. Under the circumstances, I need a favor."

"Anything."

"You know I'm taking the kids to the rodeo tomorrow night, but during the day I need to work with the foreman. Ross, will you take the kids riding? I'll get one of the staff to take the other guests fishing."

His dark brows furrowed. "Johnny's not going to like it. You know that."

"It's the only way to handle it. Tracy expects me to help make the parting easier for him. Her father-in-law let me know they're leaving for Yellowstone right after the rodeo and will be flying back to Salt Lake from there. I've decided that it'll be the best to say goodbye with a crowd around."

"I get it. Of course I'll do it. Did Tracy know they were coming?"

"I don't think so. It was supposed to be a surprise, but I can't be sure. It doesn't matter, does it? They're here, and Tracy will be leaving tomorrow for good."

The guys stared hard at him. "It *does* matter if she didn't want them to show up," Buck said.

"Want to make a bet? I spent part of the afternoon with Tony Baretta's father. He's a crusty fire chief from a long line of firefighters and he's tougher than nails. It kind of explains Tony," Carson bit out. A coughing spell followed. It was always worse for all of them this time of day. "I've got to get my inhaler. I'll see you guys later."

Carson went to his bedroom to medicate himself. After his shower, he left for Jackson to buy those chaps for Sam. He'd buy two more pair, for Rachel and Johnny, but he'd tell Monica and Tracy to hide them in their suitcases so they'd find them after they got home. The last thing he wanted was to take away the fun from Sam who'd been the winner.

He would miss those kids like crazy. It was then he realized what a huge transformation he'd undergone since Tracy had arrived. But he couldn't allow himself to think about that right now.

Later, as he was coming out of the Boot Corral with his purchases, he bumped into Carly Bishoff. "Hey, Carly." He tipped his hat to her. "How's the best barrel racer in Teton County? I hear you're going to win tomorrow night."

"You're planning to be there?"

"I am."

The good-looking redhead flashed him a winning smile. "I'd be a lot better if you ever gave me a call. I've been waiting since high school. Do you want to hook up after the rodeo?" She'd thrown that invitation out before, but he'd never taken her up on it.

"Why not?" he asked, shocking himself. It was his pain speaking, but he couldn't take it back. Tomorrow night he needed help, or he wouldn't get through it after Tracy and Johnny drove off.

"Did I hear you right, cowboy?"

"You sure did."

"Then you know where to find me after."

"It's a date."

He headed for his Jeep, already regretting what he'd done. She was a great girl. Hell and hell.

With the pizza order ready, he was able to pick it up and head straight for the Harrises' cabin. When he knocked on their door, Monica greeted him. He learned the kids had already gone and Ralph was in the shower. Carson was in luck.

"Will you hide these from Rachel until you get back to Florida? I'm giving Sam his prize tonight."

"She'll be thrilled!" Monica exclaimed. "Honestly, Carson, you've made this a dream vacation. We'll never forget."

"Neither will I, believe me. See you tomorrow when we all leave for the rodeo."

"We can't wait."

"Have fun tonight."

"Thanks to Tracy, we definitely will. She's a wonderful person."

She's more than that. "I couldn't agree more. Good night."

The children were running around outside shooting their cap guns when Carson pulled up to Tracy's cabin. The Barettas' rental car was parked along the side. They all came running up to the Jeep.

"Pizza delivery!" he called out.

The kids whooped it up and scrambled around to take the cartons inside.

"Just a minute, Sam," he called him back. "This present is for you." He handed him a sack with the chaps.

Sam looked inside and broke into a big smile. "Thanks, Carson! Wait till I show my parents!"

He ran into the cabin with Rachel and Johnny. Carson followed them. He needed to tell Tracy to come out to the Jeep so he could secretly give her Johnny's present, but she saved him the trouble by coming outside. For the moment, they were alone. She was so beautiful, he couldn't stop staring.

"H-Hi." She sounded out of breath. "I can't believe you brought pizza."

"It's a going-away party. What else could I do?"

Her hazel eyes went suspiciously bright. "Johnny's been worried about that."

He grimaced. "I haven't been too happy about it myself. What did you tell him?"

"Nothing I said has comforted him."

"He'll be all right once you're on the road with your in-laws. I bought him chaps, but I suggest you put them in the rental car so the other kids don't see them. He wanted to win."

"Johnny hasn't gotten over it. Do you know why? Because he wanted you to be proud of him."

His throat swelled. "He's the best, Tracy."

When she took the sack from him, he could feel her tremble. "Won't you stay and eat with us? Vincent said the ride was a special treat for him. That's all because of you."

"I'm glad, but didn't you know seven is a crowd when you're already a party of six?" he asked pointedly, half hoping she'd beg him to stay. But of course she didn't, and he would have been forced to turn her down anyway. "Ross will take the kids riding tomorrow. If you and your in-laws want to meet me in front of the ranch house at quarter after four, you can follow me to the rodeo grounds. It starts at five. Have a fun sleepover. If there's anything you need, call the desk. Good night."

Chapter Ten

If a horse had kicked her in the stomach, knocking her flat, Tracy couldn't have been more incapacitated as Carson got back in his Jeep and drove off without hesitation. She would never see him alone again. Being at the rodeo with him, surrounded by family and hundreds of other people, wasn't the same thing.

This was it! With children and in-laws to entertain, she couldn't run after him right now. And even if she could, what would she say? The talk with Sylvia had taken away a lot of her guilt to do with the family, but she was no closer to making a decision. Johnny was the key. She had to put him above every other consideration.

If she decided to stay on, how long would it be before Johnny wanted to go home? But if she went home, and he ended up grieving for Carson as well as his father, it could end up a nightmare.

In agony, she went back in the cabin to supervise the evening's activities.

Her in-laws stayed until it was time to get the children to bed. They planned to come by at ten tomorrow to take everyone fishing, including the Harris children who enjoyed Johnny's grandparents a lot. Sylvia and

Vincent really were the greatest. With so many grand-children, they'd had enough practice.

On the surface Johnny went along and entered into the fun as much as he could because he loved his grand-parents, but his heart wasn't in it. Tracy knew her son. The light Carson had put there had gone out again, be-cause Johnny knew they would be leaving the ranch for good tomorrow.

How much could she trust it to be a crush on Carson that he'd get over in a few weeks? Or could it be the real thing? She'd been asking herself the same question where her feelings for Carson were concerned, but the answer was easy. When he'd driven away in the Jeep, she'd felt her heart go with him. Somehow during this last week he'd stolen it from her. Now that it was his, she couldn't take it back. She didn't want to.

What if Johnny were suffering the same way? Chil-dren were so open and honest. That night at the lake after Johnny's nightmare, he'd told Carson he loved him before saying good-night. At the time, she'd assumed he'd said it because his emotions were in turmoil after such a bad dream.

But now Tracy wasn't so sure. She thought back to the many times Johnny had spent with his uncles. He loved being with them and had wonderful experiences, but she couldn't recall him ever saying he *loved* them to their faces in a one-on-one situation with no one else around. Only a certain cowboy held that honor, but he was gone.

Her thoughts came full circle to that night at the lake. When Johnny's declaration of love for Carson came blurting out, she realized it had to have been born in the deepest recesses of his soul.

With that memory weighing her down, she finally got everyone to bed. They'd planned for Rachel to sleep on the couch so Johnny and Sam could share the other bedroom. But in the end, Johnny said he wanted to sleep with her.

Rachel and Sam were happy enough to share the other bedroom. Long after the lights went out and all was quiet, she heard subdued noises coming from Johnny's bed. She listened hard. He was crying.

She raised herself up on one elbow. "That's not a happy sound I can hear. Want to talk about it?"

"No."

"No? How come?"

He turned away from her. "I just don't."

"Do you wish your grandparents hadn't come?"

"No. I'm glad they came so they could see me ride Goldie."

"They're very proud of you."

"I know."

She bit her lip, loving this wonderful son of hers who was suffering a major heartache. Trying to get to the bottom of it she said, "I bet you wish your dad could see you ride."

"Grandma says he can see me from heaven."

He'd said it so matter-of-factly, Tracy didn't know what to think. "I *know* he can, and I know he's very proud of you."

"Carson says I'm a natural. What does that mean?"

They were back to Carson. "It means you look like you were born on a horse and are getting to be an expert."

"But I won't be an expert, 'cos we're leaving tomorrow and I'll never see Goldie again. I don't want to go riding with Ross tomorrow."

"Then we don't have to."

"I don't want to go to the rodeo, either."

By now she was sitting up in her bed. "Why not?"

"I just don't."

Her spirits plunged. "But Carson's taking us."

"He can take Rachel and Sam. He likes *them*."

Tracy got out of bed and climbed into his. His pillow was wet. "Okay. Tell me what's really bothering you, honey, otherwise neither of us is going to get any sleep."

Suddenly he turned toward her and hugged her while he sobbed. Great heaving sobs that shook the bed.

"Honey—" Tracy rocked him for a long time. "What's wrong? Please tell me."

"C-Carson doesn't like me, Mom."

If the moment weren't so critical, she would have laughed. "You mean because Sam won the chaps?"

"No-o." He couldn't stop crying.

"He brought you some chaps, too, but he asked me to hide them until we got back to Ohio. It's his present to you."

"I don't want them."

"Why?"

"He only did that 'cos he thinks I'm a big baby."

"Johnny—" In her shock, she realized something deeper was going on here. "How do you know he doesn't like you?"

"He's not even going to take me riding tomorrow."

"But that's because he has ranch business."

"No, he doesn't."

"Johnny Baretta—I can't believe you just said that."

"It's true, Mom. He wouldn't stay for the party. He's

glad Grandma and Grandpa came. Now he doesn't have to be with me."

Where on earth had he gotten this idea that Carson had rejected him? Carson had done everything but stand on his head to give her son the time of his life. But since her talk with Carson the other night, plus the arrival of her in-laws, he'd backed off. *All because of you, Tracy.*

Tormented with fresh guilt, she said, "What if we weren't leaving?"

"I *want* to leave."

Since when? There was something else going on here. She would get to the bottom of it if it killed her. "Tell me the truth, honey. Did Carson do something that hurt you?"

Instead of words, more sobs answered her question. She couldn't imagine what this was all about. "I have to know, Johnny." She ached for him. "Please tell me."

Tracy had to wait to get her answer. Long after the tears dried up, she heard, "W-When I told him I loved him, he didn't tell me back."

"You mean the night when we were in the tent out camping?"

"Yes."

"But he *did* tell you."

He shot up in bed. "No, he didn't!"

"Yes he did. I remember distinctly. He said, 'The feeling's mutual, partner.'"

"What does that mean?"

Good heavens! "Honey—it meant he felt the same way."

"Then why didn't he say it?"

By now she was praying for inspiration. "Maybe he thought you weren't ready to hear the exact words back.

Maybe he was afraid you only wanted to hear those words from your father."

"Why? I *love* him! Now that Dad's gone, he's my favorite person in the whole world!"

"I know that," she said in a quiet tone, too overcome to say more.

"I wish you loved him, too." Her son's voice cracked.

Her eyes widened. "You do?"

"Yes, but I know you loved Dad and always will."

She wrapped her arm around him. "I will always love your father, but that doesn't mean I can't love someone else again one day."

He jerked back to life, sending her an unmistakable message. "It doesn't?"

"No."

"Do you think you could love Carson? I know you like him because you went to dinner with him."

Oh, Johnny... "I like him a lot."

"He likes you, too. I can tell."

Her pulse was racing. "How?"

"You know. Stuff."

"What stuff?"

"He told me you were prettier than Goldie."

"He did?" A smile found its way to her lips.

"Yup. And he said you were a better mom than any woman he had ever known. He said my dad was lucky 'cos you were the kind of a woman a man wanted to marry. But he's afraid a woman wouldn't want to marry him."

Tracy had no idea all this had gone on out of her hearing. "Why would he think that?"

"'Cos he's got a disease. He says no woman wants

to marry an old war vet who goes around coughing all the time. That's not true, is it, Mom?"

"No. Of course not. Tell you what, honey. Your grandparents flew all the way out here to be with you, so let's enjoy being with them until they have to fly home to Ohio. After we see them off at the airport, we'll bring their rental car back here and surprise Carson."

"Then we don't have to go home with them?"

"No." *Absolutely not.* "But don't let Carson know what we plan to do, otherwise it won't be a surprise."

"I *know,*" he said in that unique way of his. "Oh, Mom. I love you!" He threw his arms around her once more.

After a long hug she said, "Now it's time to sleep. We'll talk some more in the morning after the kids go home."

"Okay."

They kissed good-night and she got back in her own bed, praying for morning to get here as fast as possible. She wouldn't be able to breathe until they'd come back from Yellowstone.

AFTER THE RODEO, everyone congregated in the parking lot; the Harrises, the Barettas and Carson. The dreaded time had come for everyone to say goodbye.

"Did you like the rodeo, guys?"

"Yeah!" Sam was still jumping up and down with excitement in his jeans and chaps. "Especially the bulls!"

"They're so big!" Johnny exclaimed.

Rachel smiled up at Carson. "I liked the barrel racing. That looked so fun."

"Maybe if you keep riding after you get home to Florida, you'll be able to do it one day." He looked at the Harrises. "If you'll climb in the Jeep, I'll run you back to the ranch."

The kids all said goodbye to each other. Tracy hugged the Harrises. Carson heard them exchange email addresses. Then it was time to help her and Johnny get in the back of the Barettas' rental car. They were all packed and ready for their trip to Yellowstone.

He couldn't hug Johnny the way he wanted to, not in front of everyone. Instead, he shook his hand. "It's been a pleasure getting to know the son of Tony Baretta. We had a great time together, didn't we, partner?"

"Yup." Johnny's eyes teared up, but he didn't cry. He knew his grandparents were watching and took the parting like a man. "Thanks for everything, Carson. Be sure and give Goldie some oats for me tomorrow. Tell her I'll miss her."

"I sure will. She'll miss you, too." That boy was taking a piece of him away. Carson didn't know he could love a child this much. He shut the door and walked around to say goodbye to Tracy. She'd already gotten in but hadn't closed the door yet.

Her eyes lifted to his. "We'll never forget what you've done for us, Carson. We thanked Ross and Buck earlier, but please thank them again. You and your buddies accomplished your objective to help a grieving family heal in ways you can't possibly comprehend. Our gratitude knows no bounds."

"That's good to hear and means more than you know. We had a lot of fun, too," he said on a cough. That was the understatement of all time. Carson didn't know how much more of this he could take.

He shut her door and walked to Mr. Baretta's open

window. "There's still some daylight left, Vincent. Drive safely and enjoy."

"I'm sure we will. Thank you again, Carson. This was a great thing you did for Tracy and Johnny, one they'll remember forever." The two men shook hands.

He nodded to Sylvia. "It was a real pleasure meeting Johnny's grandmother."

"We enjoyed getting to know you, too, Carson. Goodbye and thank you."

Unable to bear it, Carson headed for his Jeep. Out of the rear window of the rental car he saw Tracy's gorgeous face. Her eyes glistened with tears. As he walked around the back end he spied Johnny's soulful brown eyes staring at him through the window. Tony Baretta's eyes. He belonged to the Baretta clan. So did Tracy.

The week from heaven had turned into the lifetime from hell.

ON MONDAY, THE family went back to watch Old Faithful go off. They'd seen it the day before, but Johnny wanted to see it again.

"Whoa!" he cried out when the geyser shot up into the air. It really was fantastic. But Tracy had something else on her mind that couldn't be put off any longer. Once they returned to Grant Village, she would have to open up the discussion that wouldn't surprise Sylvia. But it was going to shock and hurt Vincent. Luckily she knew she had her mother-in-law's blessing.

They all grabbed a bite to eat and went back to their adjoining rooms. While she was alone with Johnny, she said, "I'm going to tell your grandparents we're not going back to Ohio with them. They need to know, because we need to leave for Jackson. Your grandparents will need a good night's sleep at the motel there before they fly home tomorrow."

He jumped up and down. "I can't wait to see Carson!" He hugged her so hard, he almost knocked her over.

She needed no other answer. Though his grandparents would be leaving, the only person on his mind was Carson. She couldn't wait to see him, either. After three days' deprivation, she was dying for him.

"Okay. Let's go to their room." She tapped on the door and they told her to come in.

Sylvia was resting on the bed. Vincent sat at the table, looking at a map of Yellowstone. He glanced up. "What would you two like to do now?"

"We'd like to talk to you if it's all right." That caused her mother-in-law to sit up.

Vincent smiled. "Come on in and sit down."

"Thanks. This is hard for me to say, because I love you so much and would never want to hurt you, but I can't go back to Ohio yet. Carson has asked me and Johnny to stay on so we can get to know each other better."

"He *did?*" Johnny looked shocked.

"Yes. It was the night he took me out to dinner. I didn't tell you then, because I needed time to think about it."

But happy tears were already gushing down his cheeks. "Then he really does love us!"

"Yes. I believe he does." She had a hard time swallowing. "The problem is, we've only been here a week. That's why we need more time."

Her father-in-law stared at her. "How come it's taken

until today for you to tell us? Sylvia confided in me the other day. We've been waiting."

There was a light in his eyes, making her heart beat faster.

"Why do you think we flew out here in the first place? Natalie told us you'd met a man. When Johnny got on the phone with us, we knew it was for real. We couldn't let this go on without sizing him up."

He got to his feet and came over to hug her. "Our grandson was right. Carson Lundgren is awesome. You'd be a fool not to stay. Tony's gone, and we'll love him forever, but Sylvia and I knew this day would have to come. We just didn't know you'd fall for the king of the cowboys."

"Oh, Dad!"

It was a love fest all around with Johnny hugging his grandmother.

Three hours later, Vincent drove them to the ranch house and dropped them off in front. It was almost nine in the evening. After more hugs, kisses and promises to phone, they carried their bags into the foyer. Tracy's legs were trembling so hard, she could scarcely walk. Johnny was all decked out in his cowboy stuff.

Susan was at the front desk. When she looked up, she blinked. "Hi! We all thought you'd left! Did you leave something behind?"

Yes. Our hearts.

"As a matter of fact, we did. Is Carson around?"

"He's over at the barn with the vet. One of the horses went lame this afternoon."

Johnny stared up at Tracy. "I hope it's not Goldie."

"No," Susan said. "It's not any of the ponies."

"That's good."

Tracy smiled at Susan. "Do you mind if we leave our bags out here? We won't be long."

"Of course you can. I'll put them behind the desk for now."

"Thank you." Reaching for Johnny's hand she said, "Come on, honey. Let's go find him."

They left the ranch house at a run and kept running all the way to the barn. There was an unfamiliar truck outside. The vet's most likely. The sound of coughing let her know the location of the stall before they saw the light from it.

She ventured closer, but kept out of sight. The two men were conversing. "Let's wait till they're through," she whispered to Johnny.

Their voices drifted outside the stall. "Magpie will be all right, Carson. Let her rest for a few days, and then see if her limp is improving. This capped hock isn't serious. If she gets worse, call me."

"Will do. Thanks, Jesse."

"You bet."

Tracy and Johnny stood in the shadows. They watched the other man leave the barn. Her son looked up at her with eyes that glowed in the semidarkness. "Can I tell him we're here?" he whispered.

The blood was pounding in her ears. "Tell him whatever you want, honey."

While Tracy peeked, he moved carefully until he was behind Carson who was talking to the horse and rubbing her forelock to comfort her. What a man. What a fabulous man.

"Carson?"

He spun around so fast, Johnny backed away. The look on Carson's face was one of absolute shock.

"Johnny—" Like lightning, he hunkered down in front of her son. "What are you doing here?" His voice sounded unsteady. Closer to the source of the light, Carson showed a definite pallor.

"Mom and I decided we want to stay. Grandma and Grandpa dropped us off before they went back to Jackson."

"You mean, until tomorrow?"

"No. They're going back to Ohio. We're going to stay here. Don't you want us to?"

In the next breath Carson crushed her son in his powerful arms. "Don't I *want* you to—" he cried. "Do you have any idea how much I love you and your mom?"

"We love you, too!" came Johnny's fervent cry as he wrapped his arms tightly around Carson's neck.

"Every second since the rodeo I've been praying you'd come back."

"We would have come sooner, but we had to wait till they brought us back from Yellowstone. My grandparents think you're awesome!"

Carson's eyes played over Johnny as if he couldn't believe what he was seeing or hearing. "Where's your mom?"

Her heart almost failed her. "Right here." Tracy stepped into the light. "We came as soon as we could. It's probably too early in our relationship to be saying this, but I love you, Carson. I've known it all along, but it took Johnny to say it first. You know the old saying… a child shall lead them."

His eyes burned like the blue flames in a fire. He got to his feet. "I know the saying and believe it." She heard his sharp intake of breath. "Let's go home." His voice sounded husky as he turned off the light. Sliding an arm around her shoulders, he grasped Johnny's hand and they left the barn. "If I'm dreaming this up, then we're all in it together because I'm never letting you go."

"Is anyone using our cabin?" Johnny wanted to know.

"Yes."

"Then where will we stay?"

"With me."

Tracy's joy spiked.

"You mean in the ranch house?"

"Yup."

"Goody. I love it in there, but I've never seen where you sleep."

"You're going to find out right now, but it'll be temporary because I'm building us a house in my favorite spot by the river, smack-dab in the middle of a flowering meadow."

"You are?"

"It will have a loft where you can sleep and see the Grand Teton right out your window. I was thinking of getting a dog."

Johnny squealed. "Can I have a Boston terrier? Nate has one." Tracy didn't know that. She hadn't heard the other boy's name for a long time.

"What a great choice. He can sleep with you in the loft. You'll be able to see the mountains from every window." He squeezed Tracy's hip, sending a jolt through her like a current of electricity.

The sweet smell of sage rose up from the valley floor, increasing her euphoria. The moon had come up, distilling its serene beauty over a landscape Tracy had learned to love with a fierceness that surprised her.

When they walked in the foyer, Susan jumped to her feet. "Hi, Carson. Looks like they found you."

He sent Tracy a private message. "That they did. Just so you know, they're staying with me."

"Our luggage is behind the counter," Johnny announced. "I'll get it."

Her son was acting like a man. That was Carson's influence. He carried the cases around, but held on to the shoulder bag. Carson picked them up. "Let's go, partner. You want to open that door at the end of the hall past the restrooms?"

"Sure."

Once again Carson was allowing her into his inner sanctum, but this time there was all the difference in the world, because she wouldn't be leaving it.

He led them down a hall till he came to a bedroom on his left. "In here, Johnny. This is where you and your mom will stay for now." The room was rustic and cozy with twin beds and an en suite bathroom. Carson set the bags down on the wood floor and turned to her.

"When we planned the dude ranch, we decided we'd use this guest bedroom if there was ever an overflow. Little did I know when I sent you that letter..." He couldn't finish the sentence, but he said everything with his eyes. Her emotions were so overpowering she couldn't talk, either.

"Hey, Carson—can I see your room?"

"You bet. Follow me." They went across the hall to his suite where she'd been before. Her eyes slid to the bed where the fire between them had ignited, only to be stifled. Thank heaven this was now. The thought of another separation from Carson just meant pain to her.

"This is a big room!"

"My grandparents lived in here."

"Look at all these pictures!" Johnny ran around staring at them. "Hey, Mom—here are pictures of Carson when he was little, riding a pony like me! But there's no saddle. I want to learn to ride without a saddle. That's so cool."

"We'll try it out in a few days."

"What was your pony's name?"

"Confetti, because she was spotty."

"How cute," Tracy murmured as Carson came to stand behind her. He looped his strong arms around her neck, pressing kisses into her hair. He felt so wonderful, she couldn't wait to be alone with him.

"My grandparents took pictures of me constantly. You'll see me at every gawky stage."

"These are when you were in the Marines."

"Yup. My parents' and grandparents' pictures are on the other walls."

Johnny hurried over to look at them. "Is this your dad?"

The picture he was pointing to was in an oval frame. "Yes. He was twelve there."

"You kind of look like him."

"I've been told I resemble my mother more. See their wedding picture over on the left?"

Johnny moved to get a glance. "You do look a lot like her!"

This was an exciting night, but Johnny needed to get to bed. She needed him to go to sleep because she was going to die of longing for Carson if he didn't. "Honey? I'm sure Carson will let you look at everything tomorrow. But right now it's time for bed."

"Okay." He looked at Carson. "Will you come with me and Mom?"

"I was hoping you'd ask because I'd like to do it every night from now on. Let's go, partner."

Tracy moved ahead and pulled his pajamas out of his suitcase. Once his teeth were brushed, he climbed under the covers of the twin bed nearest the bathroom. While she stood by him, Carson set Johnny's cowboy hat on the dresser and sat down at his side.

"Do you know I never thought I'd get married or have a family?"

"I know. 'Cos you're afraid you'll cough too much and a woman won't like it, but Mom says it doesn't matter to her."

Carson shot her a penetrating glance. "Then I'm the luckiest man alive." He looked back at him. "I know I'm not your father, Johnny. I could never take his place, but I want you to know I love you as much as if you were my own son."

"I love you, too." Johnny sat up and gave him another squeeze before he settled back down against the pillow.

"Okay. It's time to go to sleep now. I'll stay with you while Carson closes up the ranch house and turns out the lights." In truth, Tracy had no idea of his routine, but until her son passed out, she couldn't go into Carson's room.

He got to his feet and tousled Johnny's hair. "I know a little filly who's going to be very happy when you show up to ride her tomorrow."

"I bet she's really missed me."

"You have no idea. Goodnight, partner. See you in the morning."

Carson's gaze slid to Tracy's. His eyes blazed with the promise of what was to come.

Chapter Eleven

Carson's elation was too great. He dashed down the hall and up the stairs. After coughing his head off, he called out to the guys. They emerged from their rooms in various states of undress.

Buck stared at him as if he were seeing an apparition. "What's happened to you? I hardly recognize the walking corpse."

"You might well ask."

"Something's up." Ross walked around him. "If I didn't know better..."

He nodded to both of them. "Tracy came back tonight with Johnny. They love me. They're here to stay and her in-laws gave us their blessing."

Slow smiles broke out on their faces. They slapped him on the back. "Congratulations. When's the wedding?"

"I haven't even been alone with her yet. She's putting Johnny to bed. I've installed them in the guest bedroom across from me. After tonight I'll know our plans better."

"What in the hell are you doing up here?"

"Trying to give her time to get him to sleep. Until we can be alone, I don't dare get anywhere near her.

Besides, the three of us have a business arrangement. I don't want you to think my personal plans change anything."

Buck nodded. "We know that."

"If you want our blessing, you've got it." Ross gave him another pat on the shoulder. "Now, you've got thirty seconds to get out of here!"

Carson's eyes smarted. "Thanks, guys. I couldn't have made it out of the hospital without you."

Ross's brow quirked. "If you didn't know it yet, you saved my life with your offer to come here."

"Amen," Buck muttered. "We were dead meat when we arrived at the hospital. It took meeting you guys to make me believe there was still some hope. If Tracy's willing to take you on, inhaler and all, then you're one lucky dude."

"She's a keeper."

"She is," Carson murmured. "Unless there's a fire, I'm unavailable till morning."

He heard hoots and wolf whistles as he started down the stairs.

TRACY HEARD HIM coming and hurried out of the bedroom. Johnny had finally dropped off. When they saw each other, they both started running. He picked her up and swung her around before carrying her into his bedroom.

"I need your mouth more than I need life," he cried softly. They mouths met and clung with a refined savagery while they tried to satisfy their hunger. But it was unquenchable as they found out when they ended up on the bed.

"Oh, Tracy..." His voice was ragged. "When you

drove away the other night, I literally thought I wasn't going to make it through the night, let alone the rest of my life. Earlier, when you told me you'd be leaving after the rodeo, I happened to meet the redheaded barrel racer in town and she asked me to meet her after it was over. I told her I would because my pain was so bad.

"But I couldn't. Instead I got a message to her that something else had come up and I went on a drive in the truck. I ended up at the pasture, if you can believe it, not even realizing where I was until I got there."

"Oh, my darling." She covered his face with kisses. "Sylvia and I had an illuminating talk before we ever left for Yellowstone. She knew what was in my heart and urged me to do what I wanted. She was wonderful. But it was Johnny who turned everything around. He said he wanted to go home because you didn't love him."

"What?"

"I know. Can you believe it? But children are so literal, and when he told you he loved you in the tent, you didn't say the same words back. He decided you didn't want him around."

"I was afraid to say it back before."

"I know. You didn't want to raise any hopes with him, and I love you for that. So when I translated what you said about the feeling being mutual, he was a changed child. I told him I loved you, too, but we needed to go to the park with his grandparents and I'd have a talk with Vincent.

"As it turned out, Sylvia had already told him the truth, and he told me I'd be a fool if I didn't stay on with you. That was music to my ears. You really did win them over, and they can see how happy you make me and Johnny. But I have to tell you, you make me so happy, I'm jumping out of my skin."

"Then jump into mine, sweetheart." They kissed over and over again, long and hard, slow and gentle, still not quite believing this was happening.

"I'm the luckiest woman alive to have met you. I don't know how I could have been so blessed.

"Besides being a hero in every sense of the word, you're absolutely the most gorgeous man, you know. I haven't been able to take my eyes off you since we got here."

"Let's talk gorgeous, shall we?" He rolled over on top of her. "That day at the lake, I could have eaten you alive."

"Then we were both having the same problem. The only trouble with falling in love when you have a son who's my shadow, is finding any time alone. Even now, he's just across the hall and could wake up at any moment."

"I know that." He ran his fingers through her silky hair. "It's probably a good thing. We need a chaperone if we're going to do this thing by the book. I've decided that's exactly what we're going to do."

"Don't I have any say in it?"

"Yes. Please don't make us wait months to get married. After what we both went through during the war, life's too precious to waste time when something this fantastic comes along. *You're* fantastic, my love."

"How about a month?"

His groan came out on a cough.

"I wish we could get married tonight, but a month will give any of the family long enough to make plans if they want to fly out for the wedding. Do you think you can wait that long?"

"I can do anything as long you'll be my wife. I guess I'd better make this official. Will you marry me, Tracy? This is going to be forever."

"Yes, yes, yes! You've made me the happiest woman on earth. Last night while I was lying in bed, tossing and turning for want of you, I started imagining married life with you. I—I always wanted another baby. A little brother or sister for Johnny, but maybe I'm getting way ahead of myself. It's just that you're already the most remarkable father to Johnny. But—"

"But what?" He stifled the word with his lips. "I think you and I were having the same dream last night, but I didn't stop with one child."

"Oh, darling—" She crushed him in her arms. "Johnny's so crazy about you. To have more babies with you— Life with you is going to be glorious!" She stared into those brilliant blue eyes. "Love me, darling. I need you so badly."

"You don't know the half of it."

Hours later, they surfaced. "Did I ever tell you the advice my grandfather gave me years ago?"

"No," she whispered into his neck.

"He told me I could look at a woman, but if she wasn't available, then that was all I could do. I'm afraid that advice got thrown out the window when you walked into the terminal."

She kissed his hard jaw. "You were inspired to invite all those special families here. It's a great thing you're doing, but I honestly believe I was guided here to you."

"I know you were. When the idea first came to me

in the hospital, it came fully fledged, like some power had planted it there."

"I believe that. I wouldn't be surprised if your grandfather had a hand in it, because he could see what was coming and wanted you to find true happiness."

"Tracy..." He murmured her name over and over. "I want to believe it because I know I've found it with you."

"I feel the same way, and I know that wherever Tony is, he's happy for us, too."

He hugged her possessively. "Don't leave me yet. We have at least an hour before sunup."

"I'll only stay a little longer, because you never know about Johnny."

"Then let's go use the other twin bed in your room, so we can enjoy this precious time without worry."

But it didn't work out so well. Carson finally fell asleep, face down, but coughed enough that by six o'clock Johnny woke up and looked over at the two of them. Tracy smiled at him. "Good morning."

"Hey—did you guys stay in here with me all night?"

Carson opened one eye and turned over. "We did for part of the night. How did you sleep, partner?"

"Good." He scrambled out of bed to get his cap gun.

"Guess what? There's a ten-year-old girl staying at your old cabin named Julie."

"Did her dad die, too?"

"No. She and her parents are tourists staying for a few days. I'm going to need you to show her how to ride."

"Has she ever been on a horse?"

"I don't know. We'll have to ask Ross."

"I think she'd better ride Mitzi."

Tracy lost the battle of tears and wiped them away furiously. "Johnny? Carson and I talked everything over last night. We're going to get married in a month."

He frowned. "How come we have to wait a month?"

Carson chuckled. "Yeah, Mom," he whispered in her ear.

"To give the family time to come if they want."

"Can I call Cory and tell him?"

"Of course. You can call everyone and invite them."

Johnny walked over to their bed. "Carson?"

By the inflection in his voice, it sounded serious. Carson sat up. "What is it?"

"When you get married, can I call you Dad?"

Carson had to clear his throat several times. "I'd be honored if you did, but only if you want to."

"I do!"

"How about if after the wedding I call you son? That's how I think of you already."

"I want to be your son," he said soberly. "Can I tell Grandma and Grandpa about…well, you know."

"Of course. I want everyone to know how happy I am."

"I'm happy, too."

"Come here, Johnny, and give me a hug."

Tracy's son flew into his arms. She sat up and threw her arms around both of them. Life simply didn't get any better than this.

* * * * *

REQUEST YOUR FREE BOOKS!
2 FREE NOVELS PLUS 2 FREE GIFTS!

HARLEQUIN

American ★ Romance®

LOVE, HOME & HAPPINESS

YES! Please send me 2 FREE Harlequin® American Romance® novels and my 2 FREE gifts (gifts are worth about $10). After receiving them, if I don't wish to receive any more books, I can return the shipping statement marked "cancel." If I don't cancel, I will receive 4 brand-new novels every month and be billed just $4.74 per book in the U.S. or $5.24 per book in Canada. That's a savings of at least 14% off the cover price! It's quite a bargain! Shipping and handling is just 50¢ per book in the U.S. and 75¢ per book in Canada.* I understand that accepting the 2 free books and gifts places me under no obligation to buy anything. I can always return a shipment and cancel at any time. Even if I never buy another book, the two free books and gifts are mine to keep forever.

154/354 HDN F4YN

Name _____ (PLEASE PRINT)

Address _____ Apt. #

City _____ State/Prov. _____ Zip/Postal Code

Signature (if under 18, a parent or guardian must sign)

Mail to the **Harlequin**® Reader Service:
IN U.S.A.: P.O. Box 1867, Buffalo, NY 14240-1867
IN CANADA: P.O. Box 609, Fort Erie, Ontario L2A 5X3

Want to try two free books from another line?
Call 1-800-873-8635 or visit www.ReaderService.com.

* Terms and prices subject to change without notice. Prices do not include applicable taxes. Sales tax applicable in N.Y. Canadian residents will be charged applicable taxes. Offer not valid in Quebec. This offer is limited to one order per household. Not valid for current subscribers to Harlequin American Romance books. All orders subject to credit approval. Credit or debit balances in a customer's account(s) may be offset by any other outstanding balance owed by or to the customer. Please allow 4 to 6 weeks for delivery. Offer available while quantities last.

Your Privacy—The Harlequin® Reader Service is committed to protecting your privacy. Our Privacy Policy is available online at www.ReaderService.com or upon request from the Harlequin Reader Service.

We make a portion of our mailing list available to reputable third parties that offer products we believe may interest you. If you prefer that we not exchange your name with third parties, or if you wish to clarify or modify your communication preferences, please visit us at www.ReaderService.com/consumerschoice or write to us at Harlequin Reader Service Preference Service, P.O. Box 9062, Buffalo, NY 14269. Include your complete name and address.

HAR13R

American ★ Romance®

A COWBOY'S PRIDE

by Pamela Britton

A wounded cowboy. His gorgeous physical
therapist. What could go wrong?

"Welcome to the New Horizons Ranch," Rana Jensen said,
tipping up on her toes in excitement.

No response.

Alana McClintock recognized Trent Anderson from watching
him on TV. It looked as if he hadn't shaved in a few days, his
jaw and chin covered by at least a week's worth of stubble.

"Good to see you, Trent," Cabe called out.

No response.

Tom hopped inside the bus and released the wheelchair. And
suddenly the longtime rodeo hero was face-to-face with the
small crowd who'd gathered to greet him.

"Welcome to New Horizons Ranch," Rana repeated happily.

Still no response.

The cowboy didn't so much as lift his head.

Tom pushed the wheelchair onto the lift. Sunlight illuminated
Trent Anderson's form. Still the same broad shoulders and
handsome face. It was his legs that looked different.

"Don't expect much of a conversation from him," said Tom.

"He hasn't spoke two words since I fetched him from the airport. Starting to think he lost his voice along with the use of his legs."

That got a reaction.

"I can still walk," Trent muttered.

Barely from what she'd heard. Partial paralysis of both legs from midthigh down. There'd been talk he'd never walk again. The fact that he had some feeling in his upper legs was a miracle.

"I'll show you to your cabin, Mr. Anderson," Rana said, coming forward.

"Don't touch me." He spun the aluminum frame around. "I can do it myself."

Alana took one look at Rana's crushed face and jumped in front of the man.

"*You* have no idea where you're going." She placed her hands on her hips and dared him to try and run her down.

"I'll find my way."

He swerved around her.

She met Cabe's gaze, then looked over at the bus driver. They both stared at her with a mix of surprise and dismay. "First cabin on the left." She stepped to the side. "Don't let the front door hit you in the butt."

Three stunned faces gazed back at her, though she didn't bother looking at Trent again. Yeah, she might have sounded harsh, but the man was a jerk.

Too bad she would have to put up with him for three weeks.

Be sure to look for A COWBOY'S PRIDE from Harlequin American Romance. Available June 4, 2013, wherever Harlequin books are sold!

HARLEQUIN®

American ★ Romance®

Peter Gladstone may have lost his beloved wife, but the
tragedy has only strengthened his resolve to create a
family. With a donor egg and a surrogate mom in place,
Peter is sure to be a proud papa soon. The only problem
is, Peter sees his egg donor Harper Anthony as a friend…
and maybe something more. And Peter has chosen to
keep his donor identity a secret. If the truth comes out,
the consequences may threaten their budding romance.
But only the truth can turn them into a family…

His Baby Dream

by JACQUELINE DIAMOND

**Available June 4 from
Harlequin® American Romance®.**

Can a stubborn cowboy let love in?
Find out in

Designs on the Cowboy
by ROXANN DELANEY

Peppy former prom queen Glory Andrews has her
work cut out building a reputation as Desperation,
Oklahoma's premier interior designer, and renovating
the century-old Walker ranch house is the first big step.
She can't fail—and she won't. Even if Dylan Walker
seems dead set against change. But Glory is determined
to show Dylan that he can let go of the past and they
can have a future together. If only the stubborn cowboy
will let her!

**Available June 4 from
Harlequin® American Romance®.**

HAR7545

HARLEQUIN®

A *Romance* FOR EVERY MOOD™

Stay up-to-date on all your
romance-reading news with the
Harlequin Shopping Guide,
featuring bestselling authors, exciting new
miniseries, books to watch and more!

The newest issue will be delivered right to you
with our compliments! There are 4 each year.

Signing up is easy.

EMAIL

ShoppingGuide@Harlequin.ca

WRITE TO US

HARLEQUIN BOOKS
Attention: Customer Service Department
P.O. Box 9057, Buffalo, NY 14269-9057

OR PHONE

1-800-873-8635 in the United States
1-888-343-9777 in Canada

Please allow 4-6 weeks for delivery of the first issue by mail.

7/14